BOURBON · PENN ·

17

March 2019

Bourbon Penn Issue 17
March 2019

Copyright © 2019 by Cognitive Wave, Inc.

www.bourbonpenn.com
Myrtle Beach, SC

Editor:
Erik Secker

Copy Editing:
J. Scott Wilson

Cover Art:
Smile
copyright © by William Basso

CONTENTS

A SONG FOR OCOTILLO

— ■ —

Kali Wallace

She had stopped watering the rose bush. Luisa had not thought about it in weeks, but she remembered it now, as she looked past the porch railing toward where the yellow blossoms drooped in the sun. It was the middle of July, but there hadn't yet been a single afternoon thunderstorm to crack the skies open. Luisa had taken it as a sign: The roses were not meant to survive.

"Look," DeeDee was saying, her smoker's voice rough over the phone, "I just thought you ought to know. He didn't say anything about, you know, bothering you. Just that he's heading back here for a while. I'll make it a short while."

Luisa said, "Thanks. I appreciate the warning."

It had been a stupid impulse to plant the roses anyway. She was surprised they had lasted this long.

"Don't you worry." DeeDee had said that two or three times already. "You give me a call if he hassles you. But he won't."

"Thanks," Luisa said again, the word fading to breath on its sibilant end.

They said their awkward goodbyes.

Staring out the kitchen window, Luisa's gaze drifted to the middle distance, the split-rail fence and white-barked aspen trees, the hillside she had looked down every day of her life blurring into an impression of summer colors. DeeDee wasn't her sister-in-law anymore, but she still tried to help. Nobody else had thought to tell Luisa that Mike was out of prison. He had served four years. The state of Colorado was satisfied with him.

Luisa focused on those sad yellow roses again. The soil over Ocotillo's grave was pale and dusty, a tan color not much different from what the horse had been in life. Around the grave, which was barren but for the roses, crisp brown grass stretched to the fence. She needed to cut it. A couple of days ago there had been a haze in the air from a fire down in New Mexico. This summer, like every summer, Colorado was only waiting its turn. To nurture a single rose plant, to flood its roots when the mountainside around it was parched, it had felt too much like shouting into a canyon, the way she had during summer trips to Mesa Verde when she was a kid, where she had done exactly that, throwing her voice recklessly against the ancient stone walls and gnarled pinyon trees, bellowing, "*Hey! Hey! Hey!*" until her parents shut her up with a root beer from the cooler in the car.

Mike was out of prison. Luisa had never felt more like shouting.

She went outside and filled a metal bucket from the spigot on the side of the cabin. Had DeeDee said he was out already, or he was getting out today? Had she mentioned how he was getting from Cañon City to Fairplay? Luisa should have listened more carefully, but her thoughts had been a beehive buzz of nerves and disappointment. Luisa had always hoped Mike would die in prison. You heard about it happening: a brawl, a stabbing with a sharpened toothbrush, and nobody shed a tear. It had been a fight that got him locked up in the first place. Not with her—the police had never cared about what he did to her—but with a group of ex-Army guys at a bar in Pueblo. During the trial, DeeDee told her that Mike's defense was that he'd been so upset Luisa was divorcing him. It wasn't so far-fetched that he might come to his end in another storm of insults and blows. The first couple of years he was locked up, she had lain awake nights wishing for a con named Bubba or Tiny or Slim—bald head, "Mom" tattoo, biceps like boulders, she saw him clearly, this simulacrum of a man—to take issue with Mike's attitude and put an end to him. But she had no such luck. You could not make a thing happen by wishing it.

Cold water overflowed the rim of the bucket. Luisa stepped back, too late, and cranked the spigot off. Drought-killed grass whipped at her soaked, squelching sneakers as she carried the water to Ocotillo's grave.

The Garcia brothers from down the road had dug the grave with their excavator. Although it had been five years, Luisa still felt the earth trembling sometimes; 1,200 pounds of 15-year-old gelding did not drop gently. The brothers had refused payment with pity in their eyes, and she had been silently relieved. At that point, before Mike's arrest, she had been terrified he would try to take her house, her land. Only when he was in prison and the divorce was final, and nothing of hers could be his anymore, had she planted the roses on Ocotillo's grave. She had not been able to bear looking at the grassy depression in the ground anymore. She had thought something beautiful and new would help.

But the scraggly bush and tattered yellow blossoms did not make the grave any less a scar on the land, and what right did she have to crave something beautiful when every summer was hotter than the last and every winter brought less and less snow? Luisa poured the water out, circling the base of the bush slowly, taking care not to wash the soil away. The dirt crumpled and darkened as it sucked in the moisture, becoming less like Ocotillo's coat and more like his mane and tail: the color of ponderosa pine bark, almost black, so dark she had felt she was braiding shadows that night she had knelt in the blood-soaked hay to cut his beautiful locks and keep them for herself.

A marriage is like a drought—somebody had said that to her once. She remembered the bitter shape of the words but not who had spoken them. You work years and years for the promise of a fruitful spring that might never come. Maybe they had said a *bad* marriage. Maybe not.

Luisa flung the last drops from the bucket and turned to leave, then stopped. A flicker of green in the soil caught her eye. A leaf—but the dirt stirred. A rise and a fall. Something was pressing upward from below.

The land was breathing.

Luisa's heart skipped. Nine feet deep. Deeper than what the county required for equine burial, the Garcias had assured her. The words had struck Luisa as so absurd she had laughed, then she had cried, pathetic, hitching sobs that made the brothers avert their eyes. Nine feet deep. For days she had thought the ground would never stop trembling. When she had realized how selfish she had been to cut Ocotillo's beautiful black mane—he had been so vain, even for a horse—she had rushed out one night to bury the coiled braids above the grave, blubbering with guilt and shame as she gave back to him what she ought never have taken. With every scoop of dirt, she had felt the trembles weaken, retreating to the roots of the mountains, to the heart of the continent, leaving nothing but the echo of a nauseating vibration in her bones. Grief and fear opened the mind to unthinkable thoughts, like a fresh wound left to suppurate and fester.

There was no tremble now. There was crumbling dirt, and there was green. Small chasms opened in the mud, revealing a tiny, gleaming black eye. It was so small, so round, so perfect. The black shine was ringed by the color of spring leaves. The eye became a head, the head a body, and the body parted into wings. A little green songbird crawled from the ground.

Luisa held her breath and leaned over for a closer look. The bird did not look injured or ill. It shook itself to shed the clinging mud and fluffed its feathers. Never taking its oil-black eye off Luisa, it crooked its head to one side, then the other. It was utterly silent. She wondered if she ought to try to capture it, to check it for hidden injury, but she had no more than twitched her fingers when the bird took to the air. Luisa felt a puff of wind and the damp kiss of a speck of dirt on her cheek. The bird whirled into the aspen grove and was soon lost among the turning silver-green leaves.

She looked eagerly to the ground again. Another glimmer of green was breaking through the mud. The second bird shoved at the soil with its beak; it had the same black eyes and green feathers. It followed the first in shaking its wings and taking to the air. Before its feet had even left the ground, a third was emerging.

Luisa counted as they emerged. There were ten, eleven, twelve, then a long, breathless pause. She could not bear that to be the last. They were such strange little creatures, so unexpected and bright as they broke free and fled to the skies. She did not want them to be gone. She watched the soil for a long time. Her breath was shallow with swallowed gasps and her skin was tingling. Birds! From the ground! She wanted to laugh with the absurdity of it. The sun was hot on her shoulders and hair, and shadows stretched as the world rolled toward night. DeeDee had called well after lunch. She had said Mike was already out—Luisa remembered now. He was out, signed through the gate a couple of days ago, and his buddy who plowed the county roads had gone to pick him up. The soil around the rosebush dried, paling from dark brown to deerskin tan once again. Luisa had dropped the empty bucket. She sat cross-legged on the ground for her vigil.

At twilight the last and littlest bird struggled from the soil. Luisa ached to help it; she did not dare. It was impossible that such a tiny thing could move the earth, but move the earth it did. It was no bigger than a hummingbird. It flapped its wings once, twice, three times. It could not fling the mud away as easily as the others. Luisa worried that it would not be able to fly. She imagined easing it into the bucket, crooning gently to soothe its panic, catching bugs to feed it—then the bird hopped in a circle, a wobbly burst of activity, and flung itself into the air. Soon it was gone like the others.

Luisa watched the sky for a long time. Evening crept over South Park, silky and purple, dry and quiet. The air cooled, the stars emerged, and the birds did not return. When she began to track satellites, and wondering if they had wings, she gave up and went inside.

• • •

The birds returned before dawn.

Luisa felt them as a fluttering at the back of her throat, as the gritty iron taste of soil on her tongue, as a puff of air from nowhere, from everywhere, teasing her hair in the curtain-dark solitude of her bedroom.

She had not slept well. Four years ago, she had bought a new mattress, new sheets, even new pillows, replacing the cheap, flat kind Mike preferred with decadent foam that cupped her head. She had given all her old linens to the senior center and carefully filled in the donation receipt. Mike had never been in this bed, but still she had dreamed about him. Not the man he had become during thirteen years of marriage, with bitterness and anger rotting him from the inside, but as he had been when they first met: 22 years old, floppy-haired, flirting with bad high school Spanish and a loose smile. In Luisa's dreams, that smiling mouth became a crumbling sinkhole, and every time it began to yawn open, she snapped awake, her entire body rigid with fear.

She heard no tires on the dirt road. No knocks at the door. No rattling of the locks. The night was quiet until dawn.

The first notes of birdsong had Luisa springing from her bed. Her bare feet found her slippers, and she shuffled swiftly through the cabin to unlock the front door. Doorknob, deadbolt, the two bolts she had installed after she kicked Mike out. Her shaking hands had been unfamiliar with the drill and unable to press the heads of the screws flush against the metal plates, but for that, at least, she had refused to ask the Garcias for help.

At this altitude, the nights were cold even in summer. Luisa stepped into a bracing morning cast in soft shades of gray beneath a blushing eastern sky: distant mountains and meadows, lakes and oxbow rivers ribboned between them, the grid of dirt roads and wire fences carving up land more empty than developed.

On the porch railing were three little birds.

They hopped along the rail, their claws dancing over the smooth log. They were fists of dark gray except for their eyes, which gleamed red. The birds were free of mud, but the tips of their wings were damp and darkened. They were as silent as ghosts, the flutter of their wings their only sound.

There was something almost like a sob, or a laugh, caught in Luisa's throat. They had come back. She had not imagined them. They had come back.

A loud grumble broke the quiet. Luisa started before she recognized the sound: the Jake brake of a truck on Highway 24, slowing for the southward curve toward Antero Reservoir.

That mechanical chatter roused the morning around her. A breeze rustled the aspens and swayed the high tops of the ponderosas around the pasture. There was a light on in the Garcias' house down the hill; their friendly, slobbering boxers began barking for breakfast. Headlights bounced along one of the arrow-straight roads below: That would be Mabel Pearson in her Ford, heading into town to open up the Shell station with a batch of fresh burritos to sell. The mountains, the valley, the morning, all of it woke as it had every other day, inevitable and familiar. The only oddity was the birds.

Two more joined the three perched on the rail. The newcomers flicked their wings, spattering the log with small, dark droplets. Luisa reached out. The birds bumped away from her, but they made no sound and they did not flee. Her fingertip came away smudged with red.

She had the outrageous urge to lick her finger, and even as the thought fluttered through her mind she tasted iron and blood: the mineral evidence of a split lip, a bitten tongue, a bloody nose draining down the back of the throat. The five birds were looking at her, every head tilted at an identical angle.

Her heart thumping, Luisa turned and retreated inside. She shut the door and leaned against it.

Nobody had come to the house in the night. Her dreams had been troubled but her safety undisturbed. There was not a sound from the little birds outside. The morning was so quiet. In her dreams, Mike had called out *hey chica, hey chica,* and the words had filled her mind with the splitting violence of summer thunder. She rubbed her thumb and forefinger together. You cannot make a thing happen by wishing it. Her pulse was footsteps, wing-beats, the clap of a spring door in a storm.

She washed her hands. She put the coffee on. She shed her robe and pajamas for jeans and a flannel shirt, traded her slippers for her stable boots, the ones she had once used for mucking stalls and shoveling manure. She clomped noisily through the cabin, not caring how much noise she made or dirt she tracked. She knew how to use a broom. She could clean, or not, whenever she wanted. She imagined Mike appearing like a phantom in the kitchen doorway—his spite-pickled older self now, not the grinning youth—with his mouth opening to snarl at her about the mess, the clutter, what was the point of having a wife if she was going to be a fucking slob, and instead of cowering and apologizing, because sometimes the right apology could forestall the blows, she let her imaginary self take the broom from the closet and snap it over her knee and drive the broken ends into his gut. She imagined the noise he would have made. She imagined scrubbing his blood from the floor. She was good at washing away bloodstains.

She poured coffee into her red mug, sweetened it with heaping spoonfuls of sugar, and carried it outside. There were seven birds now. Luisa tugged the door shut. An eighth alighted on the rail.

The morning had brightened enough that she could see the verdant green of their wings and the wet gleam at each tip, like burnished copper. She rubbed her fingers against the seam of her jeans.

Carefully, taking care not to frighten the birds, she sat down. The rocking chair had been a wedding gift from her father, built in his garage workshop before the Parkinson's had gotten too bad. Luisa had never used the chair for soothing babies to sleep, for nursing or napping, none of the things her father had wished for her. But she liked to think he would not begrudge her now, sipping her coffee as the sun rose over the Front Range, the new day a blaze of blue sky and searing mountain light.

By the time the unfamiliar Chevy Tahoe turned onto her drive, the last five birds had joined their siblings on the rail. Luisa counted them from one end to the other as they fluttered their wings and splattered the railing with dark, dark droplets. Thirteen. She could not tell which had been the last and littlest.

She didn't stand as the truck rolled to a stop, but instead stayed where she was and swallowed the dregs of lukewarm coffee from her mug. The truck had the gold star of the Park County Sheriff on its door. The officer who stepped out was a woman, tall and pale like a stalk of prairie grass, her yellow hair in a tight braid, her face leather-rough from decades in the sun.

The birds took flight as the door slammed shut. They spun upward in a dust-devil twist, out of sight, but Luisa knew when they settled on the ridge of the roof because she felt it, the prick of their damp claws, the breath-soft weight of their round bodies.

The deputy crossed the dirt driveway with an unhurried stride, and she said, "Good morning, ma'am. Are you Mrs. Egan?" She spoke with a strong Texas drawl.

Luisa said, "No. Not for five years. I'm Luisa Diego."

"Apologies, Ms. Diego. I'm Pauline Mancuso, deputy with the Park County Sheriff's Department. Mind if we have a word?"

"Did something happen?" Luisa's mouth was dry. She wondered if she ought to offer the woman some coffee. Her own mug was empty. There was only one chair on the porch.

"I'm afraid so," Mancuso said. "Sheriff Halverson asked me to stop by. I believe you know him?"

Luisa's hand tightened on her mug. "What's the problem?"

"A fisherman down at Spinney Mountain found a body by the water early this morning."

"A body," Luisa said.

"Little more than an hour ago. Right by the water," Mancuso said. "The man who found him recognized him. It's your ex-husband, Michael Egan."

"Mike," Luisa said without thinking. He hated to be called Michael. It reminded him of his mother, just like mashed potatoes, Japanese cars, the scent of lilacs in spring, women in three-quarter-length sleeves, an endless list of insignificant things he had demanded they carve out of their lives, lest a stray thought of his departed mother drift across his mind when he did not invite it. Mike's mother had died shortly after the wedding. She had been a small, frail woman with a wobbly smile that vanished when her son was looking away.

"What—" Luisa cleared her throat. The back of her tongue tasted like rust. "What happened?"

"We're trying to work that out," Mancuso said. "When was the last time you saw your ex-husband?"

Five years. A flurry of signatures. Phone calls unanswered. Heartbeats counted out like drumbeats urging an army to march. The slam of a door, any door, still reminded her of Mike storming out of the lawyer's office.

"Not since before he went to prison." Luisa weighed the risk of asking, decided it was natural to want to know. "Did somebody do something to him? Is that why you're here?"

Mancuso's eyebrows lifted. "To be honest, Ms. Diego, it's a little bit hard to tell. It looks like—well, I apologize for having to say it straight like this, but it looks like animals got to him before he was found."

"Animals?" Luisa's gaze flicked toward the dark droplets on the railing.

Mancuso followed her glance. The spots were dried now, seeped into the wood. They barely looked like blood at all. A careless splatter of wood stain—that's what she would say if the deputy asked.

But Mancuso only said, "He was sitting in a camp chair. Line set up to fish. I'm told he's always been a fisherman, and he just got out a few days ago. He might've wanted some fresh air."

He always wanted fresh air. He always wanted room to think. He wanted quiet. He wanted company. He wanted silence. He wanted conversation. He wanted freedom. He wanted affection. He was a thing made of wants, voracious, and all he ever wanted was for things to be exactly as he wanted them. The legs of his folding chair would have been sunk into the soft shore of the lake, his fishing line thin and slack over the water, like a single filament of a spider's web. Luisa could see it. She could see it so clearly she might have been standing in front of him, a flicker at the edge of his vision, a shiver of worry he would pretend not to feel. He would have his coolers beside him, one for bait and one for beer. Mesh baseball cap on his head to hide his bald spot, the tattered brim shading his face.

Whoever found him would have thought he was only dozing through a quiet morning by the water.

Hey, mister, they might have said, that unlucky person. *Hey, mister, are you okay?*

"We're trying to find anybody who can attest to his state of mind yesterday," Mancuso said.

"I haven't seen him for five years," Luisa said. "You said it was animals?"

There would have been blood, but early in the morning it might have looked like water, or piss, or spilled beer. Luisa imagined a wound in his gut. She imagined claws. She had raked her fingernails across his face once, years and years ago, one of the few times she fought back, or tried to. She had not scarred him. She had always known that was unfair, how little of what he was inside showed on the surface. In her mind the wounds in his gut changed from claw-slashes to ruptures punching through his pale skin. A man couldn't carry that much malice and not have it explode out of him in a geyser of blood and viscera. It would have hurt him more if it hadn't happened all at once. Ten, eleven, twelve ragged wounds. A long breathless pause. One more.

Deputy Mancuso was saying, "It seems that way. Would he have picked up a dog after getting out? One of those fighting dogs, maybe?"

"He hates dogs." He had been afraid of them, really, but fear turned to hate in the acid alchemy of a man's fragile pride.

Mancuso nodded. "Did you know he was back in the area?"

"DeeDee Burgess called me yesterday to say he might come back." Luisa paused. The deputy wasn't taking notes. She wasn't looking at the dark-spotted log rail anymore. "That's his sister. She lives in Alma. You should talk to her."

"Sheriff Halverson is on his way over there now," Mancuso said. "Did Mr. Egan call you when he got out of prison?"

"No," Luisa said firmly. "I wouldn't have answered if he did, but he didn't."

"The sheriff said you might say something like that," Mancuso said.

Luisa met the other woman's eyes. "I'm sure he did."

Five years ago, right after May had tipped into June, Luisa had saddled up Ocotillo and rode into the Mosquito Range for the night. She couldn't remember what Mike had said when she left, or if he'd even noticed. She had probably forgotten that very afternoon, when it was just her and Ocotillo on the trail, clomping up a snow-swollen Rough and Tumble Creek to Buffalo Meadows, where she made camp beneath peaks that became dark silhouettes as the sun set. In the cold valley bottom that rustled with wind and nocturnal animals, she had lain on the ground with her hands behind her head, listening to Ocotillo munch on spring grass and ignoring the ache in her back from the kidney blows Mike preferred—the bruises were more easily hidden than any on her face and arms. She had watched the stars emerge in the clear sky, and in that eerie, floating calm between numbness and pain she could feel the whole world, the solar system, the galaxy, everything moving and spinning, resonant and blurred like tires on sun-baked asphalt, a dizziness and a certainty she only had when she was alone. She had thought that if she shouted somebody—something—might hear. *Hey, hey.* The mountains might shout back. She had thought that she might take her horse and her truck and drive away, find a place where nobody knew her name. She had thought that when she woke in the morning, damp with dew under the golden mountain dawn, she would be different. She would know what to do. Go back to the cabin while Mike was at work. Pack a bag; she didn't need much. Load Ocotillo into the trailer. Drive until her vision blurred and her head buzzed and—there her vision stopped, because she could not imagine herself anywhere but on the land that had been her father's, and her grandmother's before him, living in the old log cabin that had become a nightmare distortion of what her home was meant to be.

When she had returned the next evening, Mike was waiting. Waiting, he said, last night for his dinner, this morning for his breakfast, and all day for his goddamned wife to do a single goddamned thing a wife was supposed to do. Luisa had ducked away from his fists, and he had laughed, a sound that sliced at her like razor blades. He told her to make dinner. He stomped outside.

Luisa was in the kitchen when she heard the gunshot from the barn.

She had called the police, but Ocotillo was dead by the time the sheriff arrived. Sheriff Halverson had shaken Mike's hand and scuffed his boots on the barn floor and said he guessed that a man taking care of his own injured livestock was no crime.

"You don't keep horses anymore?" Deputy Mancuso asked. Hers was not a voice suited to gentleness. The sheriff had sent her out here to deal with Luisa, woman to woman, but if she resented the errand, she hid it well.

Luisa looked at the barn. It needed fresh paint. Every couple of months she resolved to pay the Garcia brothers to tear it down. Every time she changed her mind.

"No," Luisa said, the word a hollow ache in her chest. She had named Ocotillo when he a foal newly dropped, because in those first wobbling hours of his life he had been tall and spindly, a little bit ugly, but beautiful too, gleaming like the first sunlight breaking through the clouds after a rainstorm.

She remembered now. It had been Mike's mother who told her about marriage and drought. Young and newlywed and gnawed by regrets, Luisa had believed the woman was scolding her to try harder. She had not recognized it as a warning.

"That's a shame. This sure is a pretty piece of property," Deputy Mancuso said.

"Is there anything else the sheriff wanted to know?" Luisa asked.

"He's not a man overly motivated by curiosity." Deputy Mancuso turned away from Luisa, looking across the driveway, over the fading yellow roses, down the sun-warmed hillside. "I'm sorry to have brought you this news so early in the morning, Ms. Diego."

After the deputy drove away, the little green birds whirled down from the roof in a single tornado flutter. They settled on the rail again. The black tips of their wings shone in the morning sun. They hopped along the log, jostling each other into a line.

Luisa counted them again: 13.

After Mike had fired the gun, after the sheriff had left, Luisa had knelt in the blood-soaked straw and cut Ocotillo's mane and tail with a sharpened kitchen knife. With every snap of blade through hair she had wished she was cutting a piece of Mike instead. The fingers of one hand, then the other, that made ten. His dick, that was eleven. A slash through his left cheek, a slash through the right, that would give him a bloody grimace where his flirtatious smile had once been. Thirteen wounds for thirteen years of marriage. When she finished, she had wiped the knife clean and put it back in the kitchen drawer.

He's gone, Luisa thought, moving her lips but making no sound. They were the same words she had whispered to herself when Mike drove his truck away in a gravel-spitting fury. When she changed the locks. When she sharpened her knives. When the bruises faded. When she walked into the lawyer's office. When she signed the papers. When she'd rid herself of his clothes, his bed, his sheets, his scent.

He's gone, she had said to herself over and over again, but every time, every time, the reassurance in her mind ended with the retort of a gunshot, the trembling of the earth, and the memory of a raw howl of grief tearing from her throat.

"He's gone," she said.

The words quivered on the morning air. The birds stilled. Their restless hopping, their careless bumping along the line, it all stopped. Thirteen pairs of red-gold eyes, thirteen sharp beaks, thirteen sets of claws stained ruddy, thirteen feathery green bodies the color of spring leaves, and not a single flicker of motion. They were all looking at her.

Luisa searched the humming cavity in her chest for guilt. She felt hollow and light, as insubstantial as dandelion fluff. If she exhaled, she would float away.

"Okay," she said. "It's okay. He's gone."

The birds tilted their heads. Then, all at once, they burst into a noisy, chattering song.

Surprised, Luisa let out a bark of laughter. The notes they sang were high and clear. They jumped from the railing to take to the air again. Luisa stood to watch them. The birds wheeled away in a loose spiral, climbing and climbing, carrying their song upward until they were no more than specks against the clear blue sky.

■

Kali Wallace studied geology and earned a PhD in geophysics before she realized she enjoyed inventing imaginary worlds more than she liked researching the real one. She is the author of the young adult novels Shallow Graves *and* The Memory Trees *and the middle grade fantasy* City of Islands. *Her first novel for adults, the sci fi thriller* Salvation Day, *will be published by Berkley in 2019. Her short fiction has appeared in Clarkesworld, F&SF, Asimov's, Tor.com, and other speculative fiction magazines. After spending most of her life in Colorado, she now lives in southern California.*

THE BONE MEN

■

George Edwards Murray

Stay awake for this, Beautiful One. Stay awake and listen.

I did not know Bone Men could feel pain until I killed one. He screamed the whole time: as he fell, as my spanner dug into his skull, as he twitched on the floor, the halo of oily blood oozing from his pearly dome. His neck-cloth fell away and his feeding-hole and breathing-hole wheezed and pulsated beneath his single row of exposed teeth. The lidless eyes rolled back and his sharp and pallid fingers scratched at the floor as he convulsed. He screamed and screamed until he gurgled into death, and the air was thick with his naked pain.

I had planned it for months. The simple act of swinging, of letting iron meet skull. Rehearsed the movement, tried to undo years of conditioning, tried to make my arm useful for something other than tightening rivets. Six months of preparation for a three-second act of rebellion and, Beautiful One, it felt like being born again.

All down the assembly line and on all the levels above and below, the other Bone Men ululated and swung their spears, viewed their fallen comrade through nets of chain-link fence and intertwining pipes. They grunted and howled. As they ran all together across the sweating pipes their naked feet made a sound like rushing water.

None of the other Workers looked up to watch me flee. Kept screwing and twisting and tightening as the assembler belched out hundreds of machine parts, inspecting and tuning each one before it continued down the line into darkness. Despite the rattles of the Bone Man dying in their midst, and the shrieks of those who pursued me, and the thunderous torrent of my panicked feet on the platform, they kept working.

All but you.

You, who stood with your spanner abandoned, smiling and holding out your hand, your eyes verdant and piercing beneath your sooty locks like opals suspended in plumes of smoke. We came together like something natural, like a drop of water falling from a pipe and plummeting to the floor. Inevitable and just right, just *right*.

We ran. Away from the line, away from the others, away from the labors assigned to us at birth. We flew into the darkness and sprinted down the catwalks suspended in the narrow tunnels, laughing, flying, each joyous footstep loosening ourselves ever more from our grim indentures. Pipes everywhere, tangled and multicolored and forming knotted walls on either side of us, some feet away from the edges of the walkway, exposing the black abyss below. But we had no fear of falling.

The Bone Men followed. Their rage echoed among the pipes. Thumping and shrieking such that the walkway vibrated. They grew louder and I realized we had nowhere to run. Where could we? The Workers' Complex? To floors above or below? The Bone Men were there. The Bone Men were everywhere. And they would find us in seconds, wrap their sharp fingers around our necks and destroy us, as they destroy all people like us, the people who upset the Way Things Are.

I stopped us in the middle of the corridor. I looked to you, and you looked around and smiled despite the onslaught of noise, the blasts of steam and cranking and the din of machination, and the hellish cries of Bone Men.

You pointed to a shadow in the pipes. You got on the guardrail and stood on it for a moment before taking off, soaring above the abyss and grabbing onto the lattice of pipes on the other side, and the last I saw was your boot sliding into darkness before you bade me to follow.

It was you, Beautiful One, who saved us. It was you who had the courage to jump.

We crawled through the tunnel of metal, laughing, banging our knees, intoxicated with rebellion. The Bone Men bellowed in frustration. They did not know to where we had escaped. Eventually the space ahead glowed orange, and as we moved forward it grew brighter, until the tunnel opened into an enormous vertical shaft. Three gigantic red pipes ran its length, beginning somewhere in the blackness above and traveling downward until they faded from view miles below our feet. Cloaking them like a sweater were hundreds, thousands, of smaller pipes, wrapped and banding together and splitting apart. Likewise the walls of the shaft were comprised of crossing, multicolored pipes, some with gauges and lamps.

And throughout this cluster of iron revolved clanking gears, their teeth interlocking in noisy fervor. Some wider than you are tall. Others the size of my thumb. Gears and pipes and more metal walkways and platforms, dancing in the shadows of the lamps, mingling and joining and separating and whirling around each other all the way up to forever, and as high as rose the furious action, so deep it fell beneath our feet. The noise was tremendous and the air smelled of oil and smoke and our eyes watered at the acrid fumes. We climbed out of the tunnel and clung to pipes and inched sideways until we reached the nearest platform.

And we ascended, and we kept alive in our hearts the legend relayed since infancy.

Topside.

The surface.

At one point you asked if I knew where the Bone Men came from. All around us the gears whirled and interlocked, indifferent to us, focused on their tasks.

They have to come from somewhere, you said.

They don't have to come from anywhere, I replied. They just are.

You said, Maybe the Bone Men have their own Complex, just like us, a wide open space in the Machine, with apartments stacked like gray blocks and each wearing a metal platform like a skirt. Only it's for Bone Men. And their women and children.

I said, I've never seen a Bone Woman.

You said, They must exist. How do you think they make more Bone Men?

I cringed but I laughed. For if there were Bone Women there surely was Bone Intercourse, and Bone Infants. The consummation of Bone Marriage. And Bone Infidelity. Bone Affairs. Bone Households feuding with Bone Neighbors. Bone Dances and Bone Requiems. Bone Happiness and Bone Sorrow. We laughed at the prospect of a life made of Bone. Bone Science. Bone Art.

And you said to me, still laughing, Can you make art?

I told you I could draw, when the supplies could be foraged. I learned by illustrating missing pages from the books which made their way into our darkness.

You said, Did you ever make anyone cry?

I said my mother once cried at one of my drawings, right before they took me away from her.

And you said, Imagine this, imagine this. A Bone Man hanging Bone Art up in his apartment. A Bone Man having tears in his eyes from a picture he hangs up in his apartment.

And you clapped your hands and giggled, and I laughed, as well.

But imagine that, Beautiful One. A Bone Man with tears in his eyes.

. . .

Please, you must listen and *remember*.

We continued upward through the network of iron, running across platforms, scaling pipes, dancing across gears in the faint light of naked bulbs. Every so often the meager cry of a Bone Man resounded from deep within the shaft, and whenever you heard it you smiled. For all their wordless lividity and fearsomeness, they could not imagine that their captives had slipped into the fabric of the Machine itself, could not imagine their charges, trained from birth for servility, now wormed through their midst, gleeful and manic and out of control. And you laughed at the thought that somewhere a Bone Man may well have been resting his gaunt foot, his heel-toe curled around, on some winding pipe which miles away ran beneath your buttocks.

You said, They are pathetic.

And I laughed, but I want to admit to you now that I was frightened. The fever of escape had broken and as we continued to climb my stomach tightened and grew heavy. I had never spent so much time away from the assembly, not even for sleep. My fingers twitched, yearned for work. Something was upset and I felt defective, like I was malfunctioning, and as the assembly line became more and more distant my state of disrepair worsened. The Bone Men had gotten inside me, had oiled and inspected and constructed me perfectly for my task.

I can't change, Beautiful One. The Bone Men had planned me so.

Although I wonder, Beautiful One, I wonder if the Bone Men had planned you entirely, planned on the gentle way your hair fell upon your shoulders, the way it caught the light in a corona which rendered your beauty ethereal. And I wonder if they planned the peculiar twist of your lips when you were thinking. The twitch of your eyebrows. The ripple of your taut muscles beneath your skin like water in a bath. I wonder if they planned on the softness of your hands. You have wondrous, delicate hands.

Beautiful One, no matter what they say, no part of them will ever live inside you.

We settled into routine. The hectic dash from platform to gear to pipe to platform became less frenetic, became calculated and familiar. We jumped over rails, passed from pipe to pipe, and scrambled across pulsing clots of gears and cogs with the same tedium as putting on our coveralls. The cries of the Bone Men were all but whispers. And our hearts simmered into embers, and we remained taciturn, except for when one warned the other:

The pipe is too hot.

That gear is slippery.

This walkway is unsteady.

The hazards of our journey became our conversation. What else were we to talk about? We shared everything else. The Bone Men planned it that way, I'm sure, to keep us from talking at the line. Standard-issue clothes. Standard-issue hair. Standard-issue apartments. Standard-issue life and standard-issue death. Raise all Workers identically and all conversation grows stale.

About every half-hour the metalwork would thin out and we would reach a more open space, and there would be a long platform which hung off the edge of the shaft and ran around its perimeter, and at different points along the platform the wall of pipes cleared and walkways trailed from the platform and into the darkness. I was on such a platform when I tried to steal some water from a pipe. My spanner was still stained with the Bone Man's blood; it blotted the pipe with black dots as I unscrewed some bolts and valves. The pipe creaked and a thread of cool water sprayed from the pipe and cascaded into the abyss.

I put my mouth to the water and drank, and was about to call you over when you ran to me, grabbed my hand and pulled me down one of the corridors. It was dark and with each turn your grip convulsed with excitement. When we reached the end of the hall, you told me to crouch down, and together we peered around the corner.

The corridor led to another platform which encircled yet another giant shaft. This one likewise was comprised of tangles of piping, but otherwise was completely empty. No gears or the like. Only the yawning abyss. A few dozen Bone Men stood on the platform, spaced evenly apart, holding spears across their sunken chests and staring down into the blackness. They gurgled and squawked softly, burbling, punctuated by gentle puffs of breath. They swayed back and forth. Sunken eyes unmoving, sallow flesh radiant in the dark. Entranced. I held my breath. We were trespassers, Beautiful One. Trespassers upon some arcane rite.

Let's go back, I said, tugging at your arm. But you would not be moved.

They're waiting for something, you said.

We watched and waited, voyeurs of this ritual, transfixed by the primal groaning of the Bone Men. My heart beat in my throat. Any second a Bone Man could turn around, look upon us with bulging, bloodshot eyes, and alert his companions. They would leap upon us and tear us apart, peeling flesh off bone with their dexterous fingers. I pictured it again and again in my head and just as I was about to break and drag you back by force, It revealed itself.

It came first by sound. Quiet, rhythmic pounding from below. Whirs and clanks atop a muddled, unbroken roar. And then louder. The Bone Men raised their spears above their heads, growled, eyes piercing, staring down at the source of the noise. The pipes shook and the catwalk bounced up and down. The lights all along the shaft switched from dull orange to flashing red as an alarm blared in syncopated shrieks. The Bone Men screamed and the rumble exploded into an earsplitting tumult that flung us to the ground.

A bronze dome crested over the platform, rising from the center of the great abyss, barely scraping past the platform upon which the Bone Men flailed and ululated and jumped. Beneath the dome hung the body of the thing, an enormous contraption made entirely of interlocking gears, springs, levers, arms, winches, chains, and all manner of mechanical viscera, moving, clicking, beating, cogs dozens of yards wide attached to cogs half their size, and those to smaller ones, and smaller again by half until they formed great fractals which shifted in and out of Its belly. All held together as if the gears were imbued with life. Skeletal arms of chrome reached out from all sides and held onto the pipes as It rose, each moving finely and with purpose like hairs in a gust of air. It reeked of oil and smoke and heat, and as its roar reached its apex and yellow light flooded the shaft, the tail of It passed before us, dangling spastic pillars of fire and belching fumes and jets of heat.

And all along the sides of It, Beautiful One, Bone Men clutched handholds, clinging like parasites. So minute, so insignificant. Yet somehow through their attachment to It, they seemed to us divine.

It rose until it was four burning spots of light above. It left nothing in its wake save awe and reverence.

We looked at each other wordlessly. Took our splayed hands from the floor and rose from our genuflections. In the presence of such wonder, mortal affectations like words are worse than useless. They are insulting, for they assume we can grasp at meaning. And this had no meaning. Or if it did it was not meant for someone like me, Beautiful One. For its vastness stretched beyond my comprehension. Before It, I am vermin.

But this is no time to discuss It, Beautiful One. Philosophy is for the privileged. All that matters is this: The device was headed Topside, and the Bone Men rode upon it. This is important for you to remember. Lock this safely away, not in your mind but in your heart. Where resides your soul, and things dwell which have no words. Where no one can touch you, no matter what else they strip away.

Beautiful One, the Bone Men can go to the surface.

Do you understand?

The Bone Men can go to the surface.

We went back to our home shaft and continued our climb. I wondered why the Bone Men had not noticed us. Perhaps they too were dumbfounded by the miracle that passed before them. Spectacular It.

Do you think the Bone Men have a sense of wonder?

Or are they too familiar with the marvels they create?

I hope you never become familiar.

By this point in our journey, another shift had almost certainly passed. I suggested we go to sleep. You scoffed at me. As if you found it amusing that I needed sleep, after what we had just seen.

Just a little further, you said, your eyes fixated on the bleeding darkness above.

And I wanted to keep going, Beautiful One, but I shook with fatigue, and my lungs burned, and gravity and weariness played tricks with my head. You, though, were radiant. I wondered then how young you really are. In the heat of our escape, and later as we ascended in the morphing shadows of the shaft, I had taken you for someone my own age. Not old but not young, either. Beaten but not dead. But the day's fervor had stripped the misery from your face and I found before me someone not much older than a child. Young and ebullient. And I realized then that I had become aged, and not only by the passage of time.

You must have seen my realization, for you said, Fine, we can sleep, and I thanked you, and we bounded across the cogs like we were one of their kin, and we rested on a platform secured to one of the main pipes.

You folded your arms and leaned against the guardrail. Nonchalantly picked off flecks of dry paint and watched them float downward through the clanking gears. You said, I will keep watch first. You sleep. And when you wake you will watch over me.

I closed my eyes and curled on the floor and fell asleep. I dreamt of dying, and when I reached my final destination, you were there waiting for me.

I woke up and you went to sleep. I paced the length of the platform as you tossed on the floor. The snarls of machinery all about us continued to knock and hum. I looked over the guardrail, to where beneath us yet more components toiled. Pockets of darkness and light commingled and danced. Efficient, cold, and exact. Illuminated spots of metal trailed down the pipes, passing in and out of sight as the manic workings of the machine covered and uncovered them with an almost-musical rhythm.

But something out of tempo stirred below.

It moved too freely, too organically to be machinery. I squinted. The dark was obscure and ever-shifting, but something below was definitely awry. I saw it then, bouncing between the gaps in the pieces.

And then came a wet and uneven chorus of moaning, and the snapping of a thousand bony claws.

I shook you awake. They've found us, I said.

We threw ourselves over the guard rail and leapt through the contraptions until we reached the edge of the shaft, affixed ourselves to the pipes and began to scramble upward. The shaft became awash with grunting, heaving, the banging of spears. The hollow pounding of ossified feet running across metal.

And their cries. Deep and trilling.

We barely touched the metal beneath our palms. Hand-over-hand like mad our feverish ascent and all around us the noise of the machinery and the Bone Men and you huffing above me and my own labored breath. Behind us they scrambled along the walls, swam through the machinery in raucous shoals. Their heads glowed: shining spheres with globular eyes. And their elongated fingers burned in the darkness like white streaks of flame. My legs shook and I sweated and slowed as each caustic breath I took set once more my lungs alight.

But Beautiful One, you never looked down. Our pursuers were beyond your fear. Beyond even contempt. You only looked up, the legend of the surface pumping beneath your skin, pulling at the fibers of your soul, its encouraging thrum supplanting the beat of your heart. As you rose I remained still, as if the Bone Men had lashed out with tendrils of fear and wrapped them around my ankles and stayed my climb.

You were almost at the next level, while I still struggled to move. You grabbed hold of the platform which encircled the shaft. And you looked down on pitiable me who quivered yards below you, my breath exploding like hot steam, flesh scalding, the shrieks of the Bone Men enveloping me, penetrating me. Undoing my joints.

Grab my hand, you said from the safety of the platform.

The shaft was saturated with howling and the rattle of claws.

I wiped the sweat from my eyes in time to see you unblemished for one last moment.

I yelled to you but you did not see until it was upon you, Beautiful One, until you half-turned and the Bone Man who had been hiding in the pipes came forth as if melting through and pierced you with his spear.

I screamed. Pushed by fear below and heartbreak above, I soared up the pipes and swung myself onto the platform as the Bone Man pulled his spear from your quivering body. You lay in blood with your hands clasped to your stomach. The Bone Man grunted and raised his spear above your head, and your eyes looked up at him bright and pleading and so radiant in the encroaching dark. I grabbed the Bone Man by the neck and we staggered across the platform, his feet scraping against metal as he made flailing kicks and flung his head back and forth and caterwauled. My hand slipped under his neckcloth and my palm brushed up against his breath-hole, which opened and closed with moist panic as I squeezed. The Bone Man tried to scream, but I wrung my hands tighter around his neck, his jawless head flailing, eyes bulging in their lidless sockets, until I brought him to the ground and grabbed his spear and rammed it so hard into his chest that it crunched through his body and rang against the metal beneath. Blood pooled around him like tarry wings. I dismounted his corpse when I stopped moving.

They coated the walls. Spread everywhere like ivory ornaments. Bleeding forth from the gears. Flying toward us.

I grabbed you and pulled your arm across my shoulders. We stumbled down the platform and turned into a corridor, you leaning ever more upon me, relying on my failing strength to hold you upright.

And you murmured, Where are we?

We are heading to the surface.

And who are you? you asked.

I just am.

You grew paler with each step, Beautiful One, and I feared I would lose you right there. The rumble of the Bone Men crescendoed behind us. Their smell flooded the hall. Decaying skin and rank fluid.

The corridor opened into a large antechamber. I laid you on the platform there. Stepping back to the corridor, I brought the spanner to each pipe I could reach, crushing the bolts in the spanner's grip and tightening each one. Dashing back and forth, the Bone Men growing louder with each desperate twist of my arm.

I stepped back as the first pallid faces turned the corner down the hall. A swarm of ashen wraiths. Some ran on all fours, abandoning their spears, clutching the ground and propelling themselves face-first. All screaming. The pipes groaned.

Hurry, hurry, I said.

The Bone Men shook their heads as they bellowed. The pipes sputtered and twanged and shook with the oncoming pressure, as closer came the thunderous mob. Just yards away. I closed my eyes.

Hurry, I said.

The pipes burst. First one, then another, blasting steam across the corridor in a wall of turbulent clouds. The Bone Men shrieked as the steam raked over their papery flesh, split it into black sores, and they all staggered back and began to babble amongst themselves. They stood there for a long while. Every so often a Bone Man would approach the searing wall, one finger out, before yelping at the heat and leaping back. They did this a few times before half the group stomped away. The rest stood and stared through the veil of chaotic whiteness.

They would soon find another entrance. Or else release the pressure in the pipes. I turned and picked you up and looked around the room. It was boxlike; metal paneling covered the walls. Some stairs led downward, and a familiar rumble emanated from below.

I think there's an assembly line in here, I said.

Though your eyes were half-closed and your face skeletal you smiled. Like where we started, you said.

I know. Let's see what's down here.

I brought you down the stairs. The floor was wet and sloshed beneath my boots. When we reached the bottom I almost dropped you to the floor.

There was an assembly line. It meandered all around the room, filling the space and leaving almost nowhere to walk. From a hole in the wall emerged the bodies of Workers. All lined up end to end. Arms and legs sticking out in all directions, soaked in blood. Some had bubbling cesspools of meat where once were faces. Others tried to hold in the entrails spilling from their abdomens. All moaned with pain. All still grotesquely alive.

At various points on the line were tunnels in which the Workers disappeared one by one. The first tunnel would click and hum and let off a cloud of steam, and then the Worker would emerge, free of injury, neat and sewn up with no scars or stitches. And after that into another machine, and there would be another series of whirs and hums and the Worker would emerge without a lower jaw. Only a gleaming row of top teeth. He would enter the next with more clicks and whirs and come out with two holes drilled into his neck. From the next he emerged with pale, hairless skin, wrapped like a cocoon. And likewise there was a machine to remove eyelids, and one to remove genitals, and one to file fingers into points.

And at the end the completed Bone Man hopped off and picked a spear from a rotating rack, and vanished into darkness. Never a hesitation. Never a refusal. The Workers became Bone Men and assumed their duties without question. Part of the larger function of the Machine, and us its gears.

I sank to my knees and set you down and vomited and wept. We became Bone Men and somewhere perhaps the Bone Men became us, as the Machine recycled us and remade us and broke our bones and rent our flesh. Endless consumption, recycling death, rebirth, transformation, for reasons beyond what our minds could comprehend.

You placed a trembling hand to my chest. Will we see the surface soon? you asked. Your voice light and cloaked in blood. Excited shrieking came from upstairs. They would come through soon.

And here, Beautiful One, is where we are.

Your breath is shallow and your skin pale. I have only one choice. I hold you over the machine. Upstairs the hiss of steam is softening. They are alleviating the pressure.

Just remember and perhaps you will not be like them. Just remember you have a choice. Remember that you can choose to be something other than a cog, a gear, a bellows, a chain.

You are not like me. You are not like anyone. You can be neither Worker nor Bone Man.

There is a gap on the belt. I undress you and set you down on it and let go. You disappear into the first machine just as the wall of steam stops hissing, and a thousand claws rattle behind me. But you have begun your transformation. They will not recognize you. You are safe.

Remember, please remember, that as they tear apart your body they cannot touch your heart, and that is where you lie. Where things dwell which have no words. Where we can make our own reasons to be.

Shrieking and footsteps and a thousand scraping fingers at my neck.

You will see the surface. Try to view it with tears in your eyes.

■

George Edwards Murray hails from Maine, where he received his MFA from the University of Southern Maine's Stonecoast program. His work has appeared in Daily Science Fiction, Gallery of Curiosities, and other publications. His online home is elegantapocalypse.com.

EXTERMINATORS

—————————— ■ ——————————

Dan Stintzi

After an eight-month stint on Mars working cargo, my company cut ties without severance and I lost my papers. I had to ship back to the moon, which was okay by me, I was tired of all the red. This was 1998 after the wars had ended. It felt like the future, even then. I found work in a maintenance facility for synthetics. It was mostly hard drive replacements and augmentations—making an arm a spatula, adding X-ray vision—handled by the med techs, and me doing clean up, squeegeeing blue fluids into drains, sorting the old parts to be recycled. I was taking a lot of daydream at the time and it was the pills that got me in touch with Harrison, who'd come back from the colonies missing a part of himself that he couldn't get back. He was half machine now and was in the habit of stealing augmentations from the rooms with keypads. He'd show up for work his normal self and by the time we clocked out he'd have a new ear that was the wrong color skin or a display window in his palm that blinked his vitals in neon green. The two of us were the same in a lot of ways.

On my third double shift in a row, ripped to high heaven, I found Harrison sorting through the to-be-burned bins, arm buried up to the elbow in a plastic tub full of spare body parts. He was far away too, waxy-eyed, moving in stop-motion. Drugs affect non-humans differently. That's what we called people like Harrison. Non-human. It's all or nothing being a person, I figure, and once you get half your brain replaced by circuit boards and gizmos or whatever, you fall sharply on the side of nothing.

He was leaned over the tub, tossing out eyeballs and fingers. "There's a piece of my brain in here somewhere."

"How's that now?"

When he was high, Harrison liked to swap out pieces without so much consideration. He often lost track of the important bits and I'd have to do some illegal operating, open up the back of his head and jam in an aftermarket replacement.

"I hear crawling. Do you hear crawling?" He turned from the tub; half his face was made of metal, which was not unusual, he'd looked like that since I'd known him, it was that it was always surprising, especially when he spun around starting with the flesh side facing you. "Don't move a goddamn muscle," he said, channeling his former self, the person who had search-and-rescued inside asteroids filled with space critters capable of slicing a guy up like deli meat.

"Look," he said pointing past me, past the doorway and into the hall at one of the security robots, a little box on wheels that had a miniature shotgun inside and had the authority to kill if it considered you troublesome. "Is that what I think it is?"

"Security?"

"I can't believe they've made it out this far."

The security robot appraised us. I lifted my badge and it blinked a couple of red lights in a way that meant it was processing and then it let out a chime like a doorbell and rolled on down the hall.

Harrison had removed his left hand at the wrist, replaced it with a star-headed drill bit. "Jesus pal, that was something else. You're lucky it didn't make you."

"The security robot?"

"You're losing it, really, truly. That thing would have sucked your brains out like a fucking milkshake."

"I don't think we're on the same page," I told him.

"We thought we got 'em all but, no, no, *nope*. And of all the places they could come to! The moon! This very fucking building! I mean, hell. I mean, I need a gun."

I spent a little time in his head after that, rooting around looking for the problem, and maybe I erased a few memories for good measure. I didn't find what was missing, but I snapped his hand back into place while he was out, and when I hit the reboot button behind his ear, he came back to me a little more levelheaded, which I needed, given the tranquilizers I had taken, the daydream still floating around my bloodstream. We had a job to do, or at least our job was creating the illusion of doing a job, and that was something we had to do together.

"I told you not to go in there anymore," he said after he powered on.

"You're not talking to me are you?" I was cleaning tools that had been used in surgery. My hands were stained with oil. "I've been doing this." There was a blot on the scalpel that wouldn't sponge off. It felt like I went at it for an hour. Our work had us mostly in the basement—the folks in charge called it sub-lunar—where time had a tendency to float around a bit.

"Do you hear crawling?" Harrison said. "When's the last time they cleaned the ducts?"

Halfway through our shift, while I was tearing strips of fake skin off a metal thigh just removed, one of the med techs, a telepath named Steve, asked me if I could find him some daydream. It was hard to lie to people who could get inside your brain, so I said sure, how much, and he told me enough to get him through the week, which was an unhelpful answer because that's not a quantity, and I said I could make it happen, and I'm sure he heard me thinking *fuck Steve all right* but he didn't say anything about it. Probably you get used to it, hearing all the horrible things people think about you.

"Is Harrison okay?" Steve said.

Harrison was behind me, sitting on an operating table, his chest cracked open and glowing digital colors. He was digging around in there with a pair of pliers.

"He's fine," I said and tried not to think my real thoughts.

"You seen any suspicious activity?" Harrison said. Little sparks shot out of his chest. "Hear anything strange?" He looked up at Steve and tapped his skin-side temple with a finger.

"I saw Doctor Marshal eat a tissue. The whole thing in one bite."

"Huh," I said.

"He didn't think anybody was watching but I saw."

"Any unusual thought patterns. I'm talking serious stuff here. I'm talking violent fantasies."

"You know as well as I do what the law has to say about sharing that stuff."

"What's the law say about daydream?" I said.

"Anybody thinking bug thoughts? Anybody thinking about the wholesale slaughter of the human race?" Harrison said.

"What?" Steve said.

I'm dealing with this, I thought, hoping Steve would hear it.

"Marigold got hit in the head by a bottle her husband threw. I heard her thinking about the sound it made. It was like *whap*." Steve pretended getting hit in the head with a bottle.

"Marigold's *fucking* husband, all right. What a *huge* surprise." Harrison's had zipped his chest back up. His human half was teary-eyed.

"You've met him?" I said.

"I've met his kind," Harrison said.

Steve said: "This is too heavy for me. Keep quiet about me telling you."

"I'd recommend preparing for the worst here. The invasion has likely already begun, aided by Marigold's husband obviously."

"Obviously," Steve said.

Really, I thought, giving him a look that said, *what the fuck, man*, forgetting that he could see inside my head.

"What we need is weapons. Like heavy artillery. You wouldn't believe how those bugs suck up rounds." Harrison was making laser sounds, firing an invisible blaster in half-circles around the room.

Oh, Jesus, I thought.

"Don't forget that daydream," Steve said.

Daydream jumbles up your body, makes your brain go kaleidoscopic. It turns toes into fingers and fingers into toes. It had been hard for me to find on Mars, but here we were swimming in the stuff. We worked and lived on the light side of the moon, the side facing Earth. The dark side folks could get fucked, in my opinion. That's where all the money was. They did their best to keep out types like Harrison and me.

We took our lunch in my buggy and bounced up and down the craters, rolled our way toward the high rises, on the way there we'd stop and meet my contact, a full synthetic named Reinhart. For lunch we had more pills, we had intergalactic visions of space gods and birds with tails made of rainbows. There was no breeze inside the containment shield, but I felt it anyway, making my hair go wavy. I was driving and the roads were mostly clear. Harrison was in the passenger seat, fully reclined and looking up at the Earth.

"Don't make me go back," he said.

"To Earth?" I said.

"Anywhere," he said, "I don't want to go anywhere ever again."

We were in Reinhart's place for all of thirty seconds when Harrison started in with the bug talk. His apartment was a closet, more or less. The three of us sat on stools in a triangle, our knees nearly touching.

"You see any creepy crawlies 'round here?" Harrison said, like we're detectives, like we were one clue away from blowing this whole thing wide open.

"I'm not sure I catch your drift," Reinhart said. His eyes blinked green. They gave off a weak light.

Figuring I could save us some time I said, "Harrison's theorizing that the bugs maybe found a way to repopulate. And now they can fly spaceships and now they are here on the moon." I looked at Harrison, "That sound right?"

"Don't forget," Harrison said, "They have human agents in their employ!"

"Far be it for me to tell people, especially you folks made out of meat, how to go about their business, but I would highly recommend that you lower your dosage." Reinhart's skin was perpetually wet-looking. His hair was made of plastic.

"Sell me the drugs now, please," I said.

Reinhart said, "Sure. Fine. Whatever."

Before we got back on the road, I opened up Harrison's head again. I wanted to find the broken pieces, make him okay, but when I went in, there was nothing wrong, the diagnostics came back clean, at least on the machine side. The human side was anybody's guess. I powered him back on and pretended like nothing was wrong.

We kept driving. I slipped into dreamland for a while, was coasting on sand along the ocean, Harrison replaced by a woman I knew once, the sun was tangled in her hair and she couldn't stop laughing, and when I came back, everything was gray and black again, and we were on the edge of containment, coming right up to the dome.

I saw two people on the outside, in a buggy like ours. They didn't have on the protective suits, so I figured they were non-human and did not need to breathe to stay alive. We got out to walk maybe fifty yards from the dome. I had to squint to make out their shapes through the glass. It became obvious to me that they were walking toward the dome, too, and might be in need of our help. I told Harrison as much and we steeled ourselves.

When we reached the glass a voice made half of static popped out a speaker painted to look like a moon rock and told us what we already knew about attempts to leave containment leading to punishments up to and including prison time.

Harrison did his best impression of the rock voice, "Do not attempt to leave your prison or you will be put in an even smaller prison."

We laughed at that for a moment, until we realized that the bodies on the other side were our own, just reflected. There was no one past containment. It was only the two of us.

• • •

We walked for a while after that, along the dome's edge. I looked up at the earth occasionally, thinking back to the places I had lived, how most of them were just places really, dirt and rock and metal, and how in each of them I had spent most of my time inside of little buildings either taking or trying to find various mind-altering substances. The earth looked like a rubber ball from where I stood, it looked like I could bounce it if I wanted to. All I had to do was reach out.

After some amount of time, Harrison and I came across a pair of chapels. They were small buildings made out of glass and they glowed from inside an off-white color. That's how I knew they were places of worship, the color of the light. I was feeling particularly reverent at the time, so I convinced Harrison that we should stop in and say a prayer. The glass walls were cloudy and I could not see through them, could not see what was happening inside.

We entered and found medical-looking tables, vats and jars filled with meats of various sizes at which were pointed industrial-sized heat lamps that buzzed and made the room feel heavy. Most of the meats were submerged in liquids or connected to long tubes that dripped out something the color of blood.

"Holy hell," Harrison approached a jug containing a three, maybe four-pound cut. He palmed his hand to the glass, wiped away the condensation. "I was right all along." He sounded elated. "This is where they do it. It's where they grow us."

"People aren't grown. People come out of other people." I did not know what purpose this meat might serve, but I knew that it was not men being made up from steaks.

Harrison fiddled with a glass instrument. He said, "People are grown! If it can be done inside a lady, it can be done inside a lab!"

"Agree to disagree," I said.

"Look, this is what's inside of you." He pointed to a fat-laced, marbled roast squeezed inside a beaker. "You are just this, but stacked up, and man oh man I've seen what happens when it comes unstacked." Something shifted in him and he started to cry. "The bugs, man. I've seen so many awful things. Every bad thing you can imagine, man, I've seen it."

Right then a bald guy in overalls came in through the back door carrying a shotgun and said, "This is private property and I am within my rights to plug the two of you right here."

"People shouldn't be grown! It's not right!" Harrison said.

"Boy, this is beef. I got all the certificates and licensures. Now do I need to repeat my previous statement, or are the two of you looking to get new holes in you?"

"I'm sorry," I said, "we ended up here by mistake."

I pulled Harrison by the arm, and we left behind the meat garden and somehow found the buggy again.

We had picked up Steve, the telepath, and we were cruising now, the three of us. I'd sold him his drugs after skimming some off the top for myself, this was standard practice and I did not feel bad about it. Harrison was driving, which was good because I was back on Mars eating a hotdog at a 4th of July barbecue. I was riding loop-de-loops on a rollercoaster singing songs I had memorized as a teenager.

We were en route to Harrison's apartment; he had something he needed to pick up. Our lunch break was an hour normally, and you could tack on a good seven, eight minutes if you got creative. Seemed like we had been gone for a day, 24 hours I mean. It's what they all still used to keep track, even on Mars. Just makes things simpler.

Steve was talking about cities back on earth I'd forgotten existed.

"Kansas City. Smog. Milwaukee. Smog. Baltimore. Smog. Every city is smog now. Tell me what you think Denver is like?"

"Smog?" I said.

"Yes. Right. Exactly. Can't see your goddamn hand in front of your face."

"Your family alive?" said Harrison. He liked to do that, zoom in the conversation, make it so people weren't sure if they should answer or not. I think he thought this made him seem like a more caring person than he was.

"No," he said. I looked back at him in the cargo bed. His pupils were black holes; they were sucking in the time and the light. "They all got burned up on a colony ship. I don't lose much sleep over it though because really, it was my grandparents that raised me."

"How is it that you don't hate people knowing what's in their minds?" I asked him. Somehow it had become Ask Steve Questions Time.

"I do hate people, mostly. Yeah, when I stop to think about it, I hate just about everybody."

"Present company excluded," Harrison said and laughed to himself. Steven didn't respond. I tried not to think anything.

• • •

Harrison's place was on the 15th story of a high rise. You could see the whole light side settlement from his window. He was in the bedroom, digging something out of the closet while Steve and I looked out. Me watching the moon ghosts rising out of the surface of the planet like a mist. Their bodies were blue outlines in the shape of people. I wasn't sure what Steve was seeing.

"You should be careful with him," Steve said. "There are dangerous things in his mind."

"Do you see the same things when you take it?" I said.

"Daydream? No," Steve said, "For me it's mostly to make the voices stop. I only hear myself when I'm on it."

"I always see the moon ghosts," I said.

Harrison returned with a duffel bag full of guns and a chunk of meat in his hand.

He said, "By the way, I stole this," and hoisted up the meat.

"Why?" I said.

"I don't know. Evidence?"

"What's the deal here?" Steve said pointing to the bag of guns.

"A contingency," Harrison said, "should our diplomatic efforts fail."

Steve was gone soon after that but I don't remember him leaving. Harrison and I were back in the buggy, him driving, with the bag of guns having replaced Steve in the cargo bed.

"Isn't this snow something?" he asked me, but I didn't see any snow, and I said, "Yeah, it's beautiful."

I woke up when the drugs had worn off, still sitting in the passenger seat of the buggy. I felt as if I was thawing out, like I'd been frozen for a generation and now the scientists had pulled my pod off the shelf and were warming up my blood. Coming down from daydream was unpleasant; it left an itching in your brain that was very hard to scratch. There was a feeling too of having been manipulated; the drug had tricked you somehow.

Harrison was smiling in a sly sort of way. He had a rifle in his lap. We were parked outside the maintenance facility where we had worked the day before. I tried to scratch the itch inside my brain and felt the metal plate on the back of my neck that I had forgotten about for a while. Daydream is capable of a lot, but the forgetting is the most important thing. The metal plate had been removed recently, I suspected, it was warm to the touch. Harrison had done some rooting around, and it was unfair of me to judge him for it, given the liberties I had taken in that department.

I too had a gun in my lap. It was a long red and black rifle. I couldn't remember how it had gotten there.

"Do you see them?" he said looking at our old building.

I looked out too, saw the gray structure in the distance, square and low, lined with yellow windows. There was movement on the landscape, fuzzy shapes crawling toward the facility. I squinted and saw the shapes become distinct, become eight-legged and many-eyed. Their legs were like razors, and I could hear the waves of tiny clicks even from the buggy. They were swarming, thick as smog as they rolled in, emerging from the cracks and craters on the moon's surface. Harrison was right. I should have never doubted him.

"What's going on?" I said. "What are we doing here?"

"Who us?" He laughed and primed the pump on his rifle like I'd seen them do in movies. It made the sound I was hoping it would. "You and me, cowboy. We're the exterminators."

■

Dan Stintzi received his MFA from Johns Hopkins University and currently lives in Wisconsin with his wife and dogs.

THE IMMATERIALISTS

■

Charles Wilkinson

"He saved the poem onto a flash drive; when he opened the document it was blank; so he went back to domain where he'd found it: nothing ... apart from an advertisement in Chinese."

The man talking to Andrew Uphill was in late middle age with a grave, lined face and cropped gray hair; he was between performances of Brecht. The tiny auditorium they were standing in had no windows and a barrel-shaped ceiling. Once Uphill had located the correct railway bridge, finding the theatre under the arches had been easy. Most of the units were bricked or boarded up; white arabesques of incomprehensible graffiti competed with multi-colored tags. A month ago, a vehicle used in a hit-and-run had been discovered in one of them. Although the theatre had no sign, there was a wicket gate in the wooden door; staple-gunned posters, badly printed in black and purple, advertised previous and present productions.

"Did he read it?" asked Uphill.

"No. He was on a computer in the Central Library and his time was almost up."

"Why did he think it was by one of Mr Zym's poets?"

"There was something about the font. He was pretty sure it was the one used by Eyam Editions."

Uphill remembered his tutor's words. *It's said there are some alive in the city who were published by Mr Zym. Most of his authors were not merely changed by the experience but altered beyond comprehension. There's a man called Richard Stack. Minor public school Marxist. Cambridge man. Radical theatre enthusiast. Directs plays in the dampest space in Europe. Watch Brenton or Edward Bond and come away with bronchial pneumonia. He used to put on poetry readings in the early seventies. Events that were well worth avoiding. He would know more about Mr Zym than I do.*

Uphill had been in the city for over a year, but his research was floundering. He'd intended to write on the British Poetry Revival in the Sixties and early Seventies, but every idea he had on the subject had already been written about. Then in the university library he came across a mention of Mr Zym in a cyclostyled magazine deep in the stacks; kaleidoscopically covered in A4 card and typed onto mauve paper; the second number of a short-lived venture , it almost came apart in his hands. Yet the vitality of those days survived in the roundup of small press publications at the back: Mr Zym's activities as a publisher were written of with the awe reserved for the hidden gods of the fugitive press.

"What happened to your friend?"

"I'm not sure. He wasn't really a friend. Just someone who used to come to a café I went to. This must have been more than ten years ago. I can't even remember his name. Of course, as a dialectical materialist, I considered his story to be nonsense," said Stack with the weary smile of one forever awaiting the final crisis of capitalism.

"You never met Mr. Zym."

"No, though his name was on the lips of the kind of confused comrade capable of reconciling shamanism with international socialism."

"I don't suppose any of these people are still around."

"I don't think so. Do you write? Apart from your academic work."

"A little ... poems. Mainly on events I feel strongly about."

"Good!"

The sound of scenery being shifted beyond the proscenium arch.

"I'm sorry," said Stack. "I'm needed soon. And no, that sort of person seldom sticks around. I'll see you out, if you don't mind. Some of the cast are oversensitive about strangers attending rehearsals."

As he was shepherded away, Uphill scribbled his email address on an envelope.   "Now I come to think of it," said Stack, opening the door, "I might have given some Eyam Editions poets a reading.   You could never tell how an event would turn out. If attendance was poor, I sometimes took pity on the poets and bought a pamphlet. I'll have a look when I've got time."

Outside, dusk collected the details from the skyline, replacing them with the orange and yellow early evening lights of the city centre. Dark furred the pale moon's edge. As he walked up the path, the dank air and softness underfoot hinted at the presence of subterranean streams, once country brooks gleaming in forgotten daylight, now flowing silently beneath the layers of compacted mud and gravel.

After reaching the main road, he hesitated, unsure of the nearest bus stop. The traffic was accelerating away from the clogged arteries around the centre. Lorries threw up a faint mist from the road; yellow headlights blossomed. There were no pedestrians on the narrow pavement. On the other side of the road was the stop where he'd alighted. He decided to walk toward the centre. It was five minutes before he came to a shelter. The frame that must once have held a timetable was empty, its remaining glass jagged and white-spidered with cracks. He tried to remember the numbers of the buses that went to the city centre. A familiar 50 rushed past without stopping, raising a web of spray. Perhaps this was a request stop. Then he became aware of another man, standing just outside the shelter, even though a fine rain had begun to fall.

"Do you know how frequent the 50s are?" Uphill asked.

The man was tall, with a closely shaven head. He was staring across in the direction of the derelict industrial buildings and wasteland of the south side, an area of darkening deprivation, illuminated only by street lighting and the traffic moving steadily toward the suburbs. The light from a passing lorry blazed on thin features tapering down to a sharp chin. Uphill was about to repeat his question, but there was something about the man's knife-like profile that forbade further interrogation. Then the bus following in its wake hissed to a stop. Without looking round, Uphill boarded.

• • •

A cloudless sky on campus, weeks before the undergraduates were due to return; yet a wash of darkness under the blue; no hint of warm hues in the red brick; even the sun-polish on the leaves brought out a trace of black in the green: It was a Midland day, far from lavish coastal light. The university was too quiet, encumbered by silence. Perhaps it was a Bank Holiday. Since leaving the station, Uphill hadn't seen a single person. Would the library be open? It seemed improbable, but as he pushed through the swinging doors, he saw a man with his back to him behind the issue desk.

He swiped his card and logged onto the library catalogue on the computer. Four titles appeared on the screen: *Beyond the Broken Forme*, *Letters on a Devil's Stick*, *The Eyam Press Book of New Poetry* and *The Eyam Press Book of Blessings & Curses*. None had a Dewey decimal number. He copied the available information and went over to the issue desk. The assistant, not one he'd seen before, was sticking orange Post-it notes onto books stacked on a white trolley.

"Excuse me," said Uphill. His voice was too loud, almost an affront to the pervasive silence. "I'm doing research on a publisher called Mr. Zym. He owned Eyam

Editions. These titles don't look as if they'll be on the open shelves."

The assistant turned around. He wore heavy black-framed glasses, which he took off, exposing two shiny red indentations on his nose. He peered at the note.

"You're right. They're in a reserved collection. Are you a student here?"

"Yes."

"You'll find them in the Stenning Room. Top floor. It's locked but I can give you a key."

"Thanks."

It was strange to have the lift to himself. As the doors closed, he felt an uncharacteristic twitch of anxiety. What if the mechanism jammed and he became stuck between floors? He'd no sooner considered the question than he reached the top level; the doors opened with a faintly ceremonial swish. Buoyed, he stepped onto the landing and followed the signs to the end of the corridor. He peered through the round window in the door and turned the key. To his right was a row of wooden carrels; three had desktop computers with blank gray-black screens. There were high rows of books in the middle of the room as well as on the walls. The sound of the strip lighting was louder here than in the corridor. Beneath the normal electrical hum came a low continuous tone he couldn't identify. He looked around for security cameras; if there were any, they weren't visible. The principle on which the books were arranged was not at once apparent. It was some time before he located the literature section. No Eyam Editions publications, as far as he could see; yet small press poetry pamphlets were sometimes found wedged between larger volumes. He'd almost completed his second search when he heard a barely discernible movement from the other side of the shelf, no greater than that made by a reader shifting his weight from one foot to the other; then the rustle of a soft hand on paper - a surreptitious turning of pages. He went around at once to the next aisle: no one - but a book slipped sideways; more swayed after it; one fell to the floor. It was as if a large volume had been plucked from the shelves, destabilizing the others. Stillness, a sense of a place suddenly vacated. Yet it was ludicrous to imagine an invisible presence was searching with him.

Uphill re-checked the literature section. *The Book of Blessings and Curses* could well be in a different section – miscellaneous, perhaps? He'd taken only a few steps toward the shelves by the door when he saw there were books on a carrel, which he was certain had been unoccupied when he came in. The chair had been moved slightly to one side, as though someone had just risen but intended to return. Uphill glanced around the room and then approached the desk. A pair of glasses and a fountain pen were resting on the pages of an open notebook. Next to it, on top of a pile of books, was *The Eyam Book of Blessings and Curses*. The buff-colored cover was faded; yet the typography remained elegant, black and exact, shining as if printed an hour ago. Uphill reached out to pick it up, when all three computers started up with a synchronous whirr; within seconds, they were blue-screened and emblazoned with icons.

Without looking back, he rushed out of the room and toward the lift. The doors were still open, as if the space inside had been primed to welcome his return. He turned and made for the stairs. As he hurtled down the levels, echoes followed him, always a footstep behind, yet so loud it seemed something heavier than himself was in pursuit. He reached the entrance hall and paused for breath; the impression of being accompanied abated. There was no one behind the issue desk. When he reached the station, he realized he'd forgotten to return the key to the Stenning Room.

Tufts of wild grass grew from gray-blue brick on top of the railway bridge. It was a surprise to see a train trundling along above him on what he'd assumed was a disused line. Uphill turned down the path to the arches. He hadn't expected a phone call from Stack so soon: "I'm afraid I haven't unearthed any of the Eyam Editions pamphlets I told you about, but I've found the journals I kept at the time I put on the readings. I'd forgotten William Timothy was published by them. He was once a friend of mine. If you come to the theatre around midday, you can take a look."

In the clear light of noon, some of the lock-ups looked less forlorn; two had been given a fresh coat of paint. The entrances of the least-favored ones, those closest to the canal, were half-obscured by hogweed and nettles. On the other side of the path was a low straggling hedge, home to discarded beer cans and crisp packets. Then beyond, an expanse of benighted brown belt: open space studded with discarded tires; gray gashes on asphalt - what must once have been a used car lot.

Uphill stepped into the gloom of the theatre. Although Stack was up on the stage, he jumped down at once, with surprising agility for a man who must have reached his seventies; he beckoned Uphill to join him by the coffee machine.

"I did put on an Eyam Editions event," he said, handing Uphill a plastic mug. "But I'd quite forgotten that William was one of the readers. He was on the fringes of the Party but not a member. What was rather unkindly referred to in those days as 'one of Lenin's useful idiots.' Bought the paper and went on a few demos – that's all."

"Is he still alive?"

"As far as I know. He had health problems. Some kind of breakdown. I visited him two or three times. He talked nonsense; that must have been why I stopped seeing him. I've only the vaguest recollection of the meetings, but it's all there in the journals."

Stack pointed to three well-bound volumes resting on a chair in the front row.

"Was he good a poet?"

"I found him incomprehensible. And the other two Eyam Editions poets were no better. It was a relief the reading was poorly attended. But you can read about it for yourself. I've marked the relevant pages."

"Did Mr. Zym turn up to support his writers?" asked Uphill, picking up the top most volume and turning the pages.

"No ... that was another thing I found surprising."

The handwriting was in black ink, elegant and italic, yet impersonal.

... it would perhaps have been too much to expect a political dimension to his poetry, but what I had failed to anticipate was the wilful obscurity of the work and how

little connection there was to the man I know. William read with toneless fluency, investing every word with equal significance. The images seemed to erase the lines before them, before themselves vanishing; there was no sense of a continuous voice: flickers of grammatical accuracy; an image that shone for a second, suggesting the emergence of meaning, then dying away before a single lucid clause could be completed. The other two were pretty much in the same vein.

Afterward, when I suggested retreating to the Shakespeare or the Trocadero, only William agreed, and then with reluctance. But once we were seated in front of two pints he recovered his characteristic animation. We must both have known the reading was a disaster, and I didn't mention it until our third pints were on the table. "I'm sorry there wasn't much of an audience," I said. "I don't suppose you sold many pamphlets. I'll buy one of yours if you've got one, even though I don't think it will contribute much to the march of history." William laughed and then said something I assumed was a joke. "I haven't any with me. Strictly speaking they exist on the verge of what's visible." Later, I remembered that I hadn't seen any of the pamphlets at the end of the reading; yet I recalled them being put out in three neat piles before the event ...

"What do you think happened to the pamphlets?"

"There was an interval. Perhaps they either sold them, which I doubt, or put them away once they realized no one was interested."

"Did you ever meet the other poets again?"

"No, I don't think so. What I know is all there in the journals. Borrow them if you wish.

Outside, the air was cooler, imbued with the imminence of rain. As Uphill stooped to find his umbrella at the bottom of his bag and then stow the journals away, he saw the grass and weeds to the side of the theatre had been flattened. Had someone had been waiting outside?

William and I decided to drive out of the city. There's a pub I know. A half-timbered ruin of a place, sawdust in the public bar, and with no sustenance other than yellow-brown pickled eggs immured in ancient vinegar. But at the back there are wooden benches in an overgrown beer garden: a good place to watch the sunset and discuss the ruined currency and the fall of governments. We had the spot to ourselves. A wind sighed in the apple tree; beyond, the fields striped and harvested, their golden parcels awaiting collection; in the distance, the hills splashed with blue shadow, crested with pink fire. As we raised our pints, the dying sun enriched the beer with gold. For once, William's normally anxious features were in repose, confident of a miracle as a knight in a Burne-Jones or Millais. "We shouldn't let ourselves be seduced by this," I told him. He turned toward me, surprised. "It's a political error," I continued, "to invest this landscape with qualities it does not have: immemorial England, intrinsically worth going to war for; home as a repository of all that is good. Like any other place, it's a built terrain, as constructed by the human hand as any suburb or inner-city slum. Examine it with an unromantic eye and you'll see exploitation in every blade of corn." He took a sip of beer. "And so now," William said, as shadows edged the stubbled fields, "even the hedgerows are involved in a political plot?" "Certainly. Their absence or presence is an indication of the extent to which the countryside has succumbed to big agriculture. In some parts of East Anglia, the fields are vast in order to maximize the profits from arable farming. But the hedgerows, though good for sparrows, were also part of the disappearance of a more communal social order." After this, we were silent for while, with only the clunk of a beer glass returned to rest on the table to disturb the silence. I sensed William had no more stomach for political talk. "What about this pamphlet of yours?" I asked. "I must confess I couldn't make much of what you read." Then he told me about Mr. Zym and Eyam Editions: "I suppose what they're looking for is poetry that cannot be paraphrased. The words engendered through the writer from a source beyond everyday discourse." I laughed: "In other words, it's completely incomprehensible. Be careful," I warned him, "that what you write is on the side of history." He replied that the fight against injustice must go on; then he added what Zym had told him: "Here there's no progression to anything but level darkness. We must feed on the light beyond." I picked up our empty glasses. "In so far as that is intelligible," I retorted, "it's an expression of a morbid, middle-class aesthetic."

It was late evening when he met the man with the shaven head on the staircase. Uphill had just returned to the block of flats where he lived alone on the top floor. In the hall, a dim yellowish cone of light on the high ceiling came on automatically. The creak of descending footsteps. It was unusual for anyone in the flats to venture out so late. The first light in the stairwell switched itself on. The hall, with its potted plant and a polished side-table on which letters for previous residents piled up, was once more submerged in gloom. An elderly couple lived on the second floor; the companionable sound of their television was just audible. As shadows reclaimed the stairs beneath him, the light on the next landing came on. For moment, he stood still, listening. Then the figure of a man emerged in front of him, slowly at first, as if developing out of photographic darkness. His close-shaven head and sharp features stirred a memory of an encounter. Uphill stepped to one side to allow him to pass. There was time to register the man was holding a parcel; then they were level. An arm brushed Uphill's chest, transmitting a faint shock like static.

While the stranger swept rapidly down the stairs, Uphill remained leaning against the wall; a few seconds ... percussive footsteps crossing the hall; then the front door unchained and banged shut. He waited. There was silence, except for voices on the television, the words indistinct.

As soon as he entered his flat, he knew someone had been in it. The light in his sitting-room was on. He went straight through. The top drawer of the desk was open and the box files, which had been stacked neatly on the bookcase, were strewn across the floor and sofa. For a moment, it seemed as if every object in the room was subtly out of place or inexpressibly different, stained by intrusion. And what if Stack's diaries had been stolen?

There were only a few more days before he was due to return them. He went straight to the bottom drawer: a familiar marbled cover. He took all three out and rifled through them - undamaged, as far as he could tell from a brief inspection.

It was midnight before he understood what had gone missing: not only the typed manuscript of the poems for his first pamphlet, but the handwritten drafts. All the Word documents and files on his computer connected to poetry had been deleted. He still had a few notebooks that contained the research for his thesis, but the sections of a first draft he'd word-processed had been wiped.

That morning he'd seen his tutor: *Your project has started to unravel since you developed this fixation with Eyam Editions, Andrew. On your own admission, the work is either no longer extant or mysteriously out on loan. Of course, there was a frisson around the name long ago, partly because it was all so secretive. But I fear it was a bubble reputation, long since popped. Why don't you go back to your first idea? Something like "The Black Mountain Poets and Their Influence on the Small Presses and Little Magazines of the West Midlands 1965 - 1975?"*

Where had he seen the man with the shaven head? The bus stop not far from the turning to the railway arches.

Then there was the parcel. Was it the right size to contain the missing manuscripts? He tried to picture the scene clearly: the tall man standing above him, his face and shoulders in darkness, the lower half of his body visible; the parcel tucked under his right arm. The shaven head, the eye riveted into angular features, the figure moving with preternatural speed past him and into the shadows beneath. And how come there was darkness above and below where Uphill stood? As if the stranger's presence was a void beneath an appearance that could never turn on the lights.

As Uphill sat on the top deck of the bus, he watched the warehouses and light industrial buildings change to red brick mansions, ornamented with a profusion of turrets and pinnacles. Then he was on the middle lane of a motorway, rushing past ribbon developments of houses with bow windows and creamy stucco facades and vast pubs in brewer's Gothic. After three changes, he alighted at a roundabout and followed a road lined with lace-curtained bungalows. Just as he thought he was lost, he reached a drive with ragged rows of rhododendrons on both sides. It was a relief to see a sign on which the name

Shady Trees had been painted. But was the place still a care home? The entry in Stack's journal, the last one to mention William, had been written thirty-five years ago:

William's sister told me he is now out of hospital and a resident of the Shady Trees Rest Home in Boundary Road. The home, which I assume to be privately run, turned out to be the very worst sort of institution of its type, more a place of last resort than recovery. I found William seated in a melancholy semi-circle; most of the other patients were in various stages of mental disintegration. He looked up from his book and smiled when he saw me, but our conversation was one-sided. He responded to nothing I said, but spoke only in low, excited tones of the activities of Eyam Editions. He appears to believe that its authors have been accorded the ability to transcend the material world. I do not think I shall visit him again.

At the end of the drive, a wild garden surrounded a white Victorian mansion, its roof suppurating with moss; the rust-red guttering and a disfigured fire-escape semi-detached from the walls. A few of the windows were boarded up. Tall trees, deciduous and dripping, grew from a ruined orangery. There was one car in a dismal asphalt forecourt. As Uphill drew closer, he saw the steering wheel was missing. He'd no expectation of finding William

Timothy alive, but had hoped the home would allow him to look at their records. It seemed inconceivable the place was inhabited. At least there was a bell push; he'd come too far not to ring it.

The door opened at once, almost before he'd taken his finger off the button. A nurse wearing a high white hat of a sort not seen on any ward for half a century appeared. An abnormally large watch with black hands and Roman numerals was pinned to her uniform.

"No visitors," she snapped.

"I haven't come to visit; this is more of a request for information. I'm researching the life of the poet William Timothy. I believe ..."

"Are you a poet?"

"Well, it's not for me ... I do try to ... now and again."

"Poets are welcome. Name?"

"Andrew Uphill."

"Come with me."

He followed her down a long, gray corridor, its linoleum floor covered in heel marks and groove-like tire tracks, as if somebody had been skidding around on gargantuan hospital trolleys. There were no pictures on the walls; not even a red fire hydrant or potted plant to measure the distance between the occasional doors. The nurse walked with gunfire footsteps, the echoes erasing every other bar of her low tuneless singing, which was either wordless or in a language unknown to Uphill. One corridor succeeded another, and then another, each presenting an identical vista. However deep they penetrated into the building, the air remained odorless, drained of all institutional smells. Once or twice, as he tried to draw level with the nurse, he would begin a sentence, only for her to accelerate away with an eerie mechanical fluidity, forcing him to break into a jog. Then at last they were at the end of the passageway and in front of a wide double door, like the entrance to a vast auditorium. The nurse stopped with a click of her heels and swung around to face him.

"The Night and Day Room," she announced. "You will find the resident within."

"You mean there's only one ..."

"We're very proud of Mr. Timothy. He has an excellent editorial eye, although of course the final decision is always Mr. Zym's."

Then she was steering him into a spacious room with high, narrow windows. White-gray spots shivered and danced in beams of subdued light. Were they motes or static from some hidden electrical source? A figure was seated in the middle of a sweep of empty floor. Uphill was halfway across the carpet when he recognized the man with the shaven head. He was older now, tucked up under a blanket, comfortable in the hide of his ancient leather armchair. Small square indentations in the carpet showed where the other seats had once stood.

"Ah, Uphill, we received your manuscript. Sorry we kept it under consideration for quite a few days. Anyway it's good news. We liked it. Although, of course, we had to make some changes to be absolutely sure you had nothing to say. Always remember that poetry isn't about meaning; it's the activity beyond the page."

"I've seen you before. Twice. But you were much younger."

"I've got the galley proofs if you'd like to take a look at them."

William Timothy reached under his blanket and drew out a pamphlet, which he handed to his visitor. From somewhere came the sound of sheets whispering through the press, the scent of invisible ink. Uphill saw his name printed on the white card of Eyam Editions. Inside there was only pagination, each number crisply printed in black, the sequencing ideal in every respect. At first, there was nothing but pure space between the endpapers: then slowly his work appeared; the act of attempted understanding lifting the words to the page.

• • •

Instead of taking the bus home, Richard Stack found himself wandering away from the city centre and through a ruined quarter of the south side, a place of abandoned factories and dusty warehouses. It was early evening, the last gold fading into the gray shadows of broken chimneys. He asked himself if he had been too much in love with dereliction: the brownfield sites; abandoned, red-brick factories with grass growing from the window frames; the hoardings tastelessly bright, squiggled with tags, an uncurated repository of urban anti-art; the whole an emblem of the end of industries, a failure of capitalism. He resented it when a street showed signs of life: an empty store reclaimed as studio space; a sandwich bar opening in a corner shop that had been abandoned for forty years; a pub that once sold sour beer refurbished and themed. To avoid passing a vintage clothes shop, he turned down an unfamiliar alley and found himself in a cul-de-sac he had never seen before. A curious cobbled courtyard surrounded by what would once have been small manufactories and workshops, some no more than large cottages, yet a spot that must once have teemed with small trades. Most of the buildings appeared abandoned, but here was one with a roof and glass in its arched windows. As he approached, he saw that a poster had been pinned to the wooden front door. Was the place some kind of meeting hall or non-conformist chapel, preserved by a few elderly worshippers? The notice was printed in a Baskerville typeface on yellow paper:

Tonight at 7:00

Eyam Editions presents

Two Radical Immaterialist Poets

Free Entry

How long was it since he'd given evidence to a police inquiry into a missing graduate student, the one who been interested in Mr. Zym? Three years at least. Now the man's name came back to him: Uphill. There'd been considerable coverage of his disappearance at the time and tearful appeals from his parents on local TV. Stack had been more co-operative with the authorities than was his custom, for he'd been keen to retrieve his diaries, but there was no trace of them - or Andrew Uphill. He peered at the notice once more. "Radical" sounded promising, but how was it possible to possess this trait and be an immaterialist? Yet whatever the quality of the poetry, which was bound to be bad, incomprehensible or both, it was possible the organizers might have information about Uphill, or even William Timothy.

He pushed the front door, which swung open at once. To his surprise, the interior consisted of a single space: a hall with galleries on either side. A smell evocative of hassocks and hymn books; no organ let alone an altar. Wooden chairs had been arranged in rows. An aisle in the middle led to a raised platform at the far end. There was nothing on it, not even a lectern and chairs for the poets. No sign of an audience. As Stack was about to sit down, a tall, thin man wearing a nondescript tweed jacket and a tie emerged from behind a screen. Although his silvery gray hair had been cut short at the side, a lock flopped over his forehead. His rimless glasses were only visible once he was standing directly in front of Stack.

"Are you here for the reading?" His voice was hushed yet clipped, like that of a museum curator.

"Yes, I hope I'm not too early."

"The event is to begin shortly."

"It's possible I may know one of the poets. Is William Timothy reading

tonight?"

"The Eyam Edition series aims to transcend the personal; the readers will remain anonymous."

"Are you Mr. Zym?"

"No, I am not."

The room darkened, only a little, but abruptly. Had a light bulb blown?

"I thought that as the publisher he might ... put in an appearance."

"Appearances are what no longer concern Mr. Zym," said the man, glancing at his watch. "I think we may as well start."

When Richard Stack sat down a few rows from the back, he became aware of a gallery above him, which presumably connected with the two at the sides. Why had he not noticed this earlier?

"Welcome to the third in this series of Eyam Editions readings," said the tall man, who was now standing at the centre of the dais. "As ever, our theme is *Words Spoken Beyond the Perceptible*. We are pleased to welcome two poets, both nameless for this evening's event. They are exponents of the School of Radical Immateriality."

Nonsense, thought Stack. What could an imperceptible performance possibly be? Perhaps he was about to be subjected to a take on John Cage's famous piece - bourgeois individualism at its very worst! And, of course, one *perceived* the passage of time, surely? Cage's title admitted as much. Marxist epistemology had no truck with the Eyam Editions' taste for self-indulgence. Perception is a form of handling; mankind has direct knowledge of reality. There is no "other country" hidden behind the veil of appearances.

He became aware of a voice above him. A poet was reciting from the gallery. In his late adolescence, an Anglo-Catholic girlfriend had taken Stack to a service in which an invisible choir sang in Latin from on high. Sickened by this display of religiosity, he'd dispensed with her affections shortly afterward. He listened to the poem. The syntax was weirdly distorted, wedded to incoherence and softly sibilant. He'd come across allegedly radical poets who claimed that the conventions of English grammar were attributes of the ruling class hegemony. To disrupt or reconstitute the ordinary sentence was in itself an act of revolutionary resistance. He was glad to say that kind of theoretical error had found no purchase at any level of the Party, let alone the branch meetings he attended; in fact, even his contributions were thought to be a touch wordy.

The room continued to darken. Only the outline of the man standing on the stage was visible. Black shapes like burnt butterflies fluttered around Stack's head. He swiped at them but failed to make contact. The voice reciting the poem grew louder, although the content was no more lucid than before. Wasn't the intonation familiar? Andrew Uphill? Yes, it was definitely him. Now a second voice joined. William Timothy. Stack recognized him at once. At first, the work was antiphonal, but slowly the volume grew, suffused with uncanny ecstasy, the voices overlapping. He could no longer see the figure on the stage.

The poets must have been reciting for over an hour. He glanced down at his watch, but could see neither its dial nor his wrist. The black space in front of him had no depth. Surely the reading must come to an end soon. It was quite absurd to sit on, uncomprehending in the triumphant dark. Were these shenanigans intended to illustrate the primacy of the word? Stack recalled Dr. Johnson's response to Bishop Berkeley's idealist philosophy: *I refute it thus*, he'd said, stamping his foot on the ground. A Tory but at least a man of sound West Midland commonsense. Stack raised his right leg and tried to slam it down. Nothing! He edged forward, angling a toecap down into a void. Then he put out a hand to touch the chair that should have been next to him. The blackness was soft and empty. "I'm sorry to interrupt," he said; "but could you turn on a light?" The voices above were no longer recognizable as those of Uphill and Timothy, although the speech retained the rhythms of a mad poetry, a patterning that seemed about to draw him into a dancing wilderness of sounds beyond the reach of ordinary words. He attempted to scream: "I really must insist ..." He could no longer hear himself speak or feel the chair that had once been so secure beneath him. The boundaries of his body were slipping away, sliding into the reaches of the level dark. If there was a gleam there, how could he tell whether it was from beyond? He was alone with the voices of perpetual performance. This was not an event it would be possible to leave.

■

Charles Wilkinson's publications include The Pain Tree and Other Stories *(London Magazine Editions, 2000). His stories have appeared in* Best Short Stories 1990 *(Heinemann),* Best English Short Stories 2 *(W.W. Norton, USA),* Best British Short Stories 2015 *(Salt), and in genre magazines/ anthologies such as* Black Static, The Dark Lane Anthology, Supernatural Tales, Theaker's Quarterly Fiction, Phantom Drift *(USA),* Bourbon Penn *(USA),* Shadows & Tall Trees *(Canada),* Nightscript *(USA) and* Best Weird Fiction 2015 *(Undertow Books, Canada). His anthologies of strange tales and weird fiction,* A Twist in the Eye *(2016) and* Splendid in Ash *(2018) appeared from Egaeus Press. A full-length collection of his poetry is forthcoming from Eyewear in 2019 and Eibonvale Press will publish his chapbook,* The January Estate, *toward the end of the same year. He lives in Wales.*

POLYDACTYL

— ■ —

Josh Pearce

Back Then

Even running flat out, you know you will not make it to the broken-down, rusting shell of the school bus before she and he do what they do. You run down the lane, skidding on the red tide of fallen autumn leaves. At the far end of the lane, you see the three remaining ruins—the church, the schoolhouse, the bunkroom of the logging camp—that form a cul-de-sac, and the bus parked in front of them. It has been there for so long that all of its windows are gone and its tires have melted away from countless summers. The three buildings are not much better off. Something terrible has happened here, long ago, turning it into a place that people tend to avoid, through unspoken unease.

Before you get there, they step out of the bus together. You are less broken by what they did than you are that she did with him and instead of with you. Examine your pain as it happens. They don't look at each other, and they don't look at you. Their eyes are deep and hollowed out like the fire-blackened door and window frames of the church.

Her knees are wobbly, an unsound foundation. The hem of her blue dress is only slightly askew, but that's askew enough for you. You take her by the hand and run away from him, away from the bus, away from the burned-out buildings. It has gotten very dark, very quickly, because of the tall trees on either side of the lane, which is within spitting distance of home but hidden by the foliage. Something terrible has happened here. As you and she run, run, run, the oaks grow long in their shadows. They are lightning-split, cored out. Some have fallen over from floodwater exposing their roots, so that it's as if you are not running through the woods, but across an ancient seabed whose water has long since dried away and surrounded you with shipwrecks. You are holding her hand and running toward what was supposed to be your future together.

Right Now

Let him in. What have you been so afraid of? He steps through the doorway and stands very close to you. All the rumors and legends you've heard about him are just that: rumors. Rumors that his fingers—at their smallest, microscopic divisions—can reach between nuclei, that he can grip your insides with van der Waals effect, that he can hold you together with strong nuclear force like nobody else in your life can or tear you down by splitting your atoms. He places his right hand on your chest, just over your heart, and your nipple reacts under his palm. With his mouth, the one in his face, he is speaking softly to reassure you that this is okay, that nothing is holding the two of you back anymore. The lips of his hand pucker around the thin cotton of your shirt, the lips of his fingers stretch all the way past your collarbone and latch onto your neck and shoulder, where they pleasurably pulse like an octopus. The lashes of all these eyes tickle your skin. The more he talks, the harder your heart beats, kicking him in the teeth.

"What can you possibly promise me?" you ask him. "We hardly know each other." The voices from his right hand are muffled when he answers. When he promises that you'll be together and that he won't let you go. "And what if you're wrong?" You look straight into his eyes, the ones that make him look human. "Can you admit, honestly, the possibility that you may be wrong? Just try it, just for a second. Entertain the notion, the barest chance, that your behavior needs changing. That there is something, anything, you could change in our interactions that would go toward making you a better person."

The last time you asked someone that exact question, she hesitated, opened her mouth a few times, and then just gave up without saying anything. It took you too long to realize that her scars couldn't change, and that maybe she was in more pain than you were. But unlike the last time you asked, the reply is immediate; he says, "I've loved you from the day you ran away." His grip on your body tightens, and you tense up in anticipation, all the kisses from all the mouths rippling up and down the points of contact. You close your eyes. And then he bites.

The palm-mouth takes the biggest piece out of you, tearing you open almost to the bone. The eyeball there is looking deep inside you. His finger-mouths rip out smaller, but still painful, chunks of flesh from your trapezius muscle, and you can feel even the tiny pinprick, mosquito-sized bites from the smaller and smaller branches of his infinite fingertips. The mouths in his left hand are singing, all together. They range up the scale quickly—you can hardly hear the uppermost pitches of the chorus coming from the finger-hands that are too small to be seen. You should be fighting him off, pushing him away, but your body is locked up completely with the sensation. The salt from his tears burns and irritates the wounds. At least you are screaming. At least you are expressing something.

Perhaps to silence you, perhaps to silence himself, the Polydactyl places the flat of his free hand over your mouth and kisses you with it. You can feel his tongue which is, indeed, bifurcated and bifurcated and bifurcated, black and swollen, filling your mouth with the topography of a Koch snowflake. You have time to think, maybe this time around won't be so bad. Maybe the scars will be worth showing off to a sympathetic audience someday, to someone who wants to see your body. Examine your pain from several dimensions as it happens. Then the Polydactyl stretches the fingers of his left hand. Two of them cover your eyes, and open wide.

Just Before

You hear a noise over the sound of the shower water pouring on your head and you freeze, blinded by rivulets of shampoo, listening for it to repeat, hoping that it won't.

It does. You open your eyes as far as the burning soap will allow, and see the Polydactyl standing on the other side of the frosted glass. You allow yourself to scream, drowning. You're angry, yes at him for getting so far in, so easily past the walls, but also at yourself for not following all the horror-movie rules of common sense. Although you'd eliminated most of the other points-of-entry to your house, you'd forgotten to replace the shower door with a curtain. Maybe you thought its transparency would save you, would make this a safe place exempt from whatever otherworldly laws the Polydactyl is living by. You put all your weight on the door so that he can't push in.

He places both hands on the glass; his hands are fractal, each finger tipped with a smaller but fully-formed hand, fully functional, and each of those has smaller finger-hands, etc., you know, the way of all such recursive things. You are used to that by now, as much as you can be. What you are not used to is the heart line of each palm opening to reveal an eyeball nestled there, and a careful observer would notice from the corner folds that they are all left eyes. His life lines have also, this entire time, been tightly clamped lips that now open to lick the moisture on the shower door with tongues the color of eggplant. You try to cover yourself with your hands, and plead, "Don't look at me!" You want to get as far away from all of those eyes while still holding the door closed. The mouths on his right hand cajole, promise, flatter. The mouths on his left hand threaten, warn, and eventually start to argue with the right hand and each other. You stick your head back under the water so that you don't have to listen, and watch the steam slowly obscure him from your sight. You eventually stop hearing the voices, and you even tune out the noise of the shower after a while, but you do hear the doorbell.

Slowly and painfully, you stand, wipe away the fog. The Polydactyl is gone, so you let yourself out. The bell rings again. You open the front door a crack to check. Your best friend is standing on the front porch, and he says, "Hi." You shut the door again quickly because the Polydactyl is standing right behind him, unnoticed. "Hello?" says a voice through the door. You pause just long enough to take a breath, and open. Still there. Close the door. Open again. Close. Finally open and there's only one man on the stoop.

"What are you doing here?" You let him in.

"You weren't answering your phone. No one's seen you in almost four days. What have you been doing?"

You shrug. "Sleeping, I guess. Taking a shower." You realize how hungry you are. He can see, on the parts of you that the robe doesn't cover, the blisters that the hot shower water burned into your skin, but he doesn't mention it as you walk to the kitchen, just sits on the couch.

"Why are all your doors out on the lawn?" You open the snack cupboard, and the Polydactyl is folded up within it, so you let the cabinet door snap back, almost crushing his fingers as he reaches out for you. Your exasperated, "Ah!" slips out, and from the other room he asks, "Okay in there?" There's always a greater-than-zero but less-than-one chance that he's behind whatever door you open, so you just have to keep opening it until the odds shift your way. Check the cabinet again. The Polydactyl is gone, so you can eat today.

Your friend sits really close to you on the couch, and you nearly jump out of your skin when he goes to take your hand. Closing your eyes, you focus on the feel of his fingers on yours, carefully counting them in your mind. He doesn't try to make any move beyond that, because you've told him all about her, about how it ended, even though you can feel in the tension of his muscles that he really wants to. You've told him about the Polydactyl, and he's told you about his jealousy of how much you talk about this mysterious man that no one else has seen, with the hint in his voice of the same bored irritation that all of your friends and family put on whenever they need to feign interest in yet another one of the new flames in your life, one who they know they'll never get the chance to meet before you've dumped them already and erased, from your vocabulary, their names. The same tone you hear when trying to get across just how omnipresent the Polydactyl is, like, for example, how he's usually waiting next to the driver's side whenever you park the car, forcing you to either drive off again or to quickly scramble out of the passenger's side and sprint for the safety of the indoors.

And, "Well," your mother repeatedly says on the phone, "it sounds like he's only trying to be a gentleman and get the door for you. Why aren't you ever interested in a nice man like that?" Because. Because he can't possibly be what he seems. Because all of the people we ever look up to or admire turn out to be false. Everyone you've ever harbored a romantic flicker for, or a man-crush, or a lady-crush, or hoped to build life with, or ever considered mating, putting a part of you into a part of them to create something that is both of you, they all end up being just too human, fatally imperfect, and by the time you realize that you shouldn't try to be like them, you already are, and that feels like someone is gnawing at the insides of your torso. You can't stand it, and you let go of his hand.

At First

The haunted place before it becomes haunted. What nature of thing has happened here to turn it into a desolate ruin, visited only by teenage misfits and adults with questionable motives? Local speculation disagrees: Maybe it was that week a false storm covered the city, lightning without thunder, blackout clouds with no rain; or when the Perseids were especially thick, falling as constant as hail. A piece broke off of the sky and struck the church, setting it ablaze—retribution, went the whispers, from God because the minister had been secretly sacrificing his congregation in blood rituals. Likely something more mundane, you figure from your local history classes, like the over-logging whose legacy, decades after the camp was bankrupted by the violent government suppression of a union strike, of loosened soil washes the lane away in landslides every first rain of the season.

You go to that school for a single year, and your lack of popularity certainly has something to do with the sense of alienation of this place. You are the weird kid, sitting alone at lunch, picking at the warts on your hands while the other students play tag and skip rope and tell each other ghost stories about a serial killer who gouges his victims' eyes out with his thumbs and dumps their empty skulls among the fields of tree stumps that are just over there, they point, on the other side of the hill, across the street. There is a newspaper article in the school library, dated 1929, about logger Jerome O'Brian, who reported finding something out in the woods that was neither human nor animal but, when authorities investigated the spot, had already disappeared, dragging itself into the underbrush, and no amount of dedicated forestry ever uncovered it again.

Who knows. Maybe the terrible thing has always been here. You look across the lunchroom and notice her for the first time, wearing blue. She looks at you and smiles. Examine this moment from multiple dimensions as it happens. Listen to the shrieks of your classmates—they sound like your mother and father fighting down the hall, like your mother and her boyfriend fucking when you walk, quickly, head down, from the front door to lock yourself in your room. Listen to their voices mingling— they sound like the overheard gossip at the begrudgingly attended sleepover birthday parties as you go into the bathroom and shut the door that is thinner than everyone else suspects it is. You look away, and look back. She is still there, and still smiling. Look away again, and look back. Still smiling. One more time. She is still there, but no longer smiling. Can you imagine yourself with this person? Can you picture the two of you behind closed doors?

You cross your fingers and go to talk to her. You have time to think, maybe this time around won't be so bad.

∎

Josh Pearce's writing is published in Analog, Asimov's, Beneath Ceaseless Skies, Clarkesworld, InterGalactic Medicine Show, *and* Nature *magazine. You can find more on his website, fictionaljosh.com, or on Twitter: @fictionaljosh. He has five fingers on each hand.*

RITUALS

—————— ■ ——————

Hamdy Elgammal

1.

Monday morning, it's Mindy's turn on the leash.

She strips off her gown and Nurse ties the leash around her waist. She gets down on all fours. Mindy's breasts hang below her. She barks at a slender old man opposite her. When she is done barking, Nurse says, "Flail," so she flails. Her toes flex against the floor. Nurse says, "Scream," and she screams a wet and tired sound.

The old man is dressed in khakis and a bloodstained sweater. He crosses his arms, smiles, puts them down then crosses them again. He does this over and over but he never talks. The Machine's projections don't talk.

Nurse says, "Breathe," and Mindy inhales, takes off the leash and puts her gown back on. She walks out and comes to sit beside me.

"Well done," I tell Mindy.

"Water," she croaks.

I give her my bottle and she drinks. She keeps her head down, staring at her hands, folded in her lap. I put my hand on top of hers, feel her roughness under my fingertips. She cries and I hold her. "You can cry if it's your first time," I say. "I cried my first time. It's fine."

"It's what he did when he showed the police the grave." Mindy says. "He was proud of it, the grave he dug for my Teddy."

I close my eyes, catch myself trying not to think of graves or dead children. Four months I've been here now. Four months, one week, two days.

I touch her wrist, feel her pulse is up, say, "You'll be just fine."

"This is hell," she says.

"Not quite," I say.

Through the one-way mirror on the leash room, we watch the remaining mothers take turns. They bark, flail, scream. Then they come around and sit next to us. Mindy and I watch as the Machine's holograms morph into a pit bull with a foaming mouth. Then the pit bull's face melts and becomes a bus bumper with bits of someone on its grill. Then the grill grows a tap and becomes an overflowing bathtub. The bathtub grows tentacles and morphs into a large brain tumor.

When all the mothers have taken their turn, Nurse switches off the Machine and everything quiets down. She walks back and stands before us with her clipboard. She's wearing bright white shoes.

"Bedtime," she says and we walk to the dorm.

I can never sleep these days. Mindy's bunk is next to mine. She stares at the empty bunk above her.

"Karen, you're a good person," she says.

"Thanks, I guess."

I always have a hard time with Mindy's bedtime conversations.

She asks, "Is the worst of it over?"

I shut my eyes, feel a tear against an eyelid. I hold Mindy's hand.

2.

Thursday night is Purge Night. Nurse seats us in glass boxes, four to a box, each in a corner. The glass is cold against my bare skin. Nurse says, "Purge," and we bang our hands against the glass.

We bang until someone breaks the glass in each box and it turns red with blood.

I break the glass in my box. Warm blood runs down my palms. "Up," Nurse says and I rise and step out of my box and walk to Nurse. I start to cry then I wipe my eyes. Nurse holds a small mirror to my face. There is blood on my forehead and my cheeks, straight lines down and across from wiping my face with bloodied hands. It looks like the face of a warrior from some Amazonian tribe. For a moment, this calms me.

Nurse puts the mirror away then touches a small glass canister against my cheek, trapping my tears into it. She caps the canister and stashes it in her pocket.

"Where do they go?" she asks for the millionth time.

"In the water, in the water we drink."

"Why do they go there?"

"Because they're good for you."

That night, when everyone is sleeping, I sneak back into the leash room. When I enter, the leash is folded on the table, the Machine next to it whirs like a refrigerator. I fidget with the bandage on my hand then sit on the floor.

The Machine emits a small whistle before a beam of light hits my face. I sit and stare at my own eyes. My projection is me and I'm wearing a blue dress with a cloud pattern. When Alex first spoke, he had pointed to that dress and said, "Sky."

"I hate you." I tell the projection. It doesn't respond; this is a one-way conversation.

Four months ago, when I first arrived at LeaveBehind, Nurse asked about my pick for the Machine.

"Can it be me?" I asked.

"It's a difficult decision, who to blame for the broken things inside us." Nurse said. "You can pick yourself but maybe we put some makeup on the projection to assist you during the more intense sessions."

"No," I interrupted her, "no disguises."

Nurse shrugged, wrote "self" on her clipboard. Then she repeated the motto of the facility.

"All it takes is a step forward."

3.

A List of Things You Will Throw Out

His old coloring books (outlines of black parrots, pink rabbits, all messy inside), his crayons, his schoolbag (empty out crumbs and all that sand), his water bottle, his Star Wars bed sheets smelling like lilac (keep just this one thing?), his shoes (fidget with the Post-It on the garbage bag that says: "Goodwill"), all his books full of wicked witches and giants and talking goats, his Legos, his underwear with the bad elastic, his height chart and Oddball, the duck in armor with a frayed tail ("I found a name, I found a name, I found a name! Wanna hear it? Sir Oddball the Frayed! Ha! Ha ha ha!").

His blank notebooks, lined up to be filled.

His toothbrush.

His comb (keep the hair, you get to keep those strands, that's him now, can't throw him out).

4.

Next morning, Nurse walks into the dorm wearing her anger mask. It's plastic and white with frowning eyebrows, holes for eyes and a mouth cut out in the shape of a bowtie.

"Who entered the leash room last night?" she says.

Nobody replies. I sit there, trying to maintain a neutral expression. Nurse comes over to me and asks, "Was it you, Karen?"

"No," I say.

"Karen," she says.

I look at her mask, chew on my lower lip.

"I know it was you."

"It wasn't me." I say.

Nurse slaps me.

"No!" I say, tears in my eyes.

She walks over to Mindy's chair, says, "Mindy will be disciplined if you do not admit. Was it you, Karen?"

"Why punish Mindy?" I say.

The room is silent. I can hear my own heartbeat.

"It was! It *was* her, it was her!" says Mindy from the far end of the row.

I look at Mindy and her eyes are wide, her fingers tugging on Nurse's sleeve.

"I need to hear it from Karen," says Nurse as she looks at me. In her anger mask, I can't help but think that she looks like the kind of person who would wind up on the Machine someday, be someone's living, looping nightmare to flail at.

"It was me," I say.

"Why did you do it?" Nurse asks.

I don't say anything so she presses on, "Did you want some alone time with the Machine?"

"Yes," I say.

"Hand," she says and I look at her.

"Please," I say.

She cocks her head sideways, eyes still fixed on mine. I close my eyes then extend my arm and she holds on to it, fingers cold around my skin. From her scrub pocket, she takes a small syringe and injects me with it. It's a small prick at first and I can feel the warm serum coursing up my inner elbow. Tonight, I realize, my dreams will *really* suck.

"No alone time except under supervision and with the leash, Karen." Nurse says.

I sob. She sighs then moves over to my chair, pats my back. "We're heading to the yard," she says to everyone.

She takes off the anger mask on our way out.

When we're out, Nurse stands with a clipboard at one end of the yard and the rest of us stand next to each other. In front of us is a row of identical little girls. All of them have the same short black hair, the same neutral faces, dead as Styrofoam cups. They're dressed in hospital gowns and a little whiteboard dangles around each of their necks by a string. Each whiteboard has one of our names scrawled on.

Nurse says, "Move," and each row moves a few steps closer to the other until we are a step away.

"Don't be afraid of getting close to your inner child," Nurse says.

My inner girl's sign has my name misspelled (KARN). It's written in yellow crayon so bright that I can barely see it in the afternoon sun. We stand in front of each other. I point at her with my index finger, she touches her index finger against mine, her eyes turning a bright silver.

"How have you been?" KARN asks.

"I'm well," I say. "I'm old."

"You are *very* old," she says. "How does it feel to be so old?"

"Not super-old. Oldish. 32."

"Are you happy?"

"What do you mean?"

"Let me show you." Then she steps away and does a little *changement* that I used to do when I was nine. I find it quite moving, how she knows to do a *changement*, how she thinks that is happy.

"How do you know how to do that?" I ask.

She points to her left wrist where a barcode is tattooed.

I bend down, wrap my arms around her. Against my knees, the yard's grass is rough and plastic. I wish she would melt into me, somehow. When I pull back, a strand of my hair is tangled in hers and we straighten it out.

"Do you have something to tell me?" KARN asks.

"Mindy ratted me out today."

"You were already caught."

"How do you know?"

"Same way I know how to do a *changement*."

I reach to stroke her hair then reconsider, hover my hand above her head, strands of her hair tickle my palm.

"Where do you go?" I ask. "After I get out of here, where do you go?"

She tilts her head up toward the sky where some ducks fly by. I watch them with her. They ascend, descend and ascend again, up and down like a yo-yo.

"Home," she answers.

"Where is that?"

"Where you stop running from yourself."

"Isn't that line from a fucking TV show?"

"Hey! *Karen!*" Nurse shouts. "You can't say 'fucking' in front of your inner child!"

KARN and I roll our eyes.

KARN gives Nurse a side-eye, then, under her breath, she says, "You just *said* 'fucking.' Dumb cunt."

I giggle. KARN grins.

"Where do *you* go when you get out of here?" KARN asks.

I can't find an answer. I pretend I'm thinking something profound, fix my eyes on those ducks.

5.

**Some Questions You Will Remember Given
the Right Drug**

What – what car accident? What do you mean "identify
the body?" When? How?

What food do we get for the funeral? Which coffin?

What face to wear?

Who will be at the funeral? Why do they get to smile
and cry and say they are sorry for my loss? Why is there
no hand around *their* lungs, squeezing the air out of them
with each breath?

How is he now my "loss?"

Can we cancel the funeral? Why are there funerals?

Why now?

Is he in the ground? Is he in these fucking pictures?

Did it hurt?

Why us?

Why me?

6.

A week later, Nurse comes into our dorm, says, "Karen,
Mindy, your first assessments are next Thursday."

A passed assessment means we get out. A failed one is a month's extension. Every mother's assessment is different. Mindy sits up in her bunk, facing me.

"I'm sorry," she says, "about the other day."

I study her face. She has pockmarks on her nose and her left cheek. Her lips are parched and her eyes are dry. Somewhere under there, there was once a person. Now there's only skin and imperfections. I wonder how my face looks, if it has melted away yet.

"It's okay," I say, "I forgive you." I move over to sit on the bunk next to her.

"Do you think we'll pass the assessment?" she says.

"I'm not sure. Do you want to get out?"

"I don't know."

"What do you think it's going to be like, getting out?" I ask Mindy. She's silent, maybe she's thinking, but I can't stand silence anymore. Not today. I want to open my chest and lay my red heart in her lap and have her feel everything inside. Here Mindy, I'd say, tell me something good.

Instead, I put my hand on her head and push her face against my chest, feel our collective lungs breathing like a machine.

7.

Bed Sheet

THERAPIST OFFICE INTERIOR, MORNING.

KAREN seated on one side of the office, holding onto a child-sized black sneaker. THERAPIST is sitting on opposite end of the office next to a small table. In the background is a big, circular, colored glass window with the outline of a white swan drawn against a blue backdrop. Daylight shines through it. Center is ALEX who lies face-up, head at KAREN's side and feet at THERAPIST's. His eyes are closed and there's blood pooling around his head.

In both of KAREN's and THERAPIST's laps are their own hearts, red and pulsing, dripping blood down on the floor and their clothes. Their hearts are connected to their bodies at their chest with two plastic tubes that go under their shirts.

KAREN: Some days it's like every angle I see is slightly off by a few degrees. As if everything I own, my couch, my toothbrush, the little cherub figurine on my bookshelf had been stolen and then replaced with an exact replica. Some days it feels like I'm stuck in a bag of skin. Like I, too, am a copy of someone else who used to live in this body. That doesn't make sense. I don't know.

THERAPIST: Go on.

KAREN: I think what hurts the most is forgetting. Because it's not in my control and because I'm forgetting already. Last Thursday, I was at the supermarket, shopping for groceries. When I got home I realized I had only got my Captain Crunch and not Alex's Fruit Loops. I didn't even think twice about it at the cereal aisle or at the cash register or on the way home. Only when I was unpacking the shopping bags. Then last Friday, somebody sent me a cat video and – well, I laughed. I felt so guilty about laughing and right after, I tried to remember Alex's laugh, the sound of it. But I couldn't. In my head, it was just this silent loop of him laughing, as if someone had pressed the mute button. So I said words I associated with his laugh out loud to myself instead: "Warm, comfortable, loved." I could put words to the memory but the thing itself was gone.

THERAPIST: *(puts his hand on the heart in his lap as if petting it)* That all sounds very hard.

KAREN: I always heard people talking about grief. I used to think of it as some sort of extra-sad sadness. But I don't think it's that.

THERAPIST: What do you think it is?

KAREN: A kind of death.

(KAREN pinches one of the tubes connecting her heart to the rest of her body. Her heart struggles in its pulse. Then she lets it go and the heart goes back to normal.)

THERAPIST: Have you had thoughts about hurting yourself or others?

KAREN: If I say yes, you'll just put me away someplace.

THERAPIST: I can't put you anywhere you don't want to be. You never gave me that authority.

(Silence)

THERAPIST: *(crosses one leg over another)* What's with the shoe?

KAREN: I got it back from Goodwill. I couldn't find the other half of the pair, though.

THERAPIST: Do you like holding it?

KAREN: *(nods)*

THERAPIST: How is your sleep?

KAREN: Bad.

THERAPIST: Ambien?

KAREN: Mostly. I got a few hours last night though, at least.

THERAPIST: Did you do anything different last night or just the Ambien?

KAREN: Knitting.

THERAPIST: *(surprised, smiles)* Well that sounds – interesting.

KAREN: *(laughs weakly)* Yeah.

THERAPIST: What are you knitting?

KAREN: Knitt*ed*. I knitted all of Alex's old clothes together. The ones, you know – the ones I couldn't give away. I made a bed sheet.

THERAPIST: *(concerned)* From Alex's old clothes?

KAREN: *(excited)* Well I stayed up all night. I joined each pajama top and bottom, each pair of pants, T-shirt, underwear, everything. There was even this red onesie with white dinosaurs on it from when he was two. It didn't all fit perfectly together. But I filled up the spaces with his old socks. It's uneven and patchy in places but now I have a bed sheet. Of him. I spread it on my bed when I was done and fell, face-first, onto it.

(THERAPIST stands, carefully holding his heart in one hand, and walks to the desk behind him and grabs a brochure. KAREN, looking directly at ALEX and not noticing THERAPIST walking, continues talking.)

KAREN: I put my nose against each part the sheet and I inhaled – his body lotion, his sweat, his powder, some of it years old. I breathed until it felt like he was closer to me than my own veins. Then I looked at the wall clock and saw it was 4 a.m and I slept.

(THERAPIST returns to foreground.)

THERAPIST: Alright, I have a suggestion. Take it or leave it, no pressure. This is a new experimental place. *(He steps over ALEX and hands KAREN the brochure.)* A change of scenery.

8.

The night before our assessment, Mindy gets her hands on a box of cigarettes and I convince her to sneak up to the roof to smoke with me.

I'm wearing only my nightgown and it's cold up there. Every gust of wind seems to pierce a bone. There are broken chair legs on one side and a bucket of paint on the other. Someone has painted the word "Forgiven?" in bright yellow paint on the far wall.

"Forgiven?" Mindy reads.

"Forgiven," I say, like I mean it.

We sit on the wall and dangle our legs in the air. Mindy lights up and passes me the cigarette. The warm smoke fills my lungs, rushes past my nostrils on its way out. Then Mindy gets up and stands on the wall. She stretches her hands to her side. Her gown is stuck to the front of her body by the wind.

"All it takes," she says, giggling slightly, "is a step forward."

Mindy puts one foot out, arms still outstretched.

"Get down, Mindy," I say, trying to mask the panic in my voice.

But then, the wind rubs my hair a certain way and something changes. I put out the cigarette.

I get up and I stand a little farther on the edge and stretch my arms until my fingertips touch Mindy's. I dangle one foot out.

"There." I say, catching my breath. "Now, what?"

9.

Day Of

Usually you drive Alex to school but not this morning. This morning you are lazy.

You wake up crummy; two pounds heavier on the scale. The bus stop is only a couple of blocks away, he'd taken it before to school. You say, "Honey, do you mind taking the bus today?"

He sighs, says, "Lazy Karen."

"Hey!" you say, smiling.

He leaves his cereal half-eaten and heads for the door. Before he goes out he stops, as if he remembered something. He holds the door, grins at the street outside then turns to you. This is the picture: him holding the door ajar, smiling like he has a secret.

"Forget anything?" you ask as you pick up the dishes.

"Nope." he says. "Drink your coffee Lazy Karen."

Then you hear the sound of the screen door shutting behind him, his footsteps on the stairs.

You're still at the kitchen table, smoking a cigarette, when the phone rings.

10.

Nurse wakes us up the next morning and leads us to the yard. Outside, the morning is all clear sky and clueless birds. A wooden wall, as wide as the yard and as tall as the building, stands across the grass. At its center is an orange nylon tube, with only its rim visible, big enough for a person to walk into.

"You go first, Karen." Nurse says to me. "You get in the tube, get out the other side. If you take longer than fifteen minutes, you fail."

"That's it?"

Nurse nods. I look to Mindy.

"Good luck," Mindy mouths at me.

I take a step inside. The nylon is soft against my fingertips. I look behind me and the tube has already closed my entrance, the rim no longer visible from inside.

Then my legs give way and I'm on my knees. There is no other way to navigate. The tube seems to be pressing shut in front of me and I have to pry it open with my arms.

I look behind me for Mindy, but I see nothing except the shifting nylon, closed in from both sides. I push open more space and keep staggering along. Through the folds I can only glimpse what's ahead.

Just enough to keep on, keep pushing against these shifting walls.

Fall. Get up. Fall better.

It's hard, lonely work.

Far but inching close is the other side of the yard. I see flickers; jagged coins of tender light dancing softly, softly, on the cold, dead grass.

∎

Hamdy Elgammal is an Egyptian software engineer and writer based in Berkeley, CA. For a few years in middle-school he wrote Harry Potter fan fiction but he's since moved on. His prose has been published or is forthcoming in Origins Journal, Jersey Devil Press, Easy Street *and* Five on the Fifth.

RAVENOUS MERMAIDS

———————— ■ ————————

Dawn Sperber

This bridge drips rain in my hair, cold drops that wind down my scalp, cold snakes.

It's still a good home. Shade over my head and the rushing creek down below. This creek winds all through the woods and feeds into the pond. It tells me tales, unheard secrets. No one knows all the water stories I know.

No one else has escaped the mermaid's teeth.

Makes you charmed, I'd say, to touch an iridescent face, feel their soft lips (how do they not bite their lips?), to see their razor teeth and get away.

I've seen them eat dogs before.

• • •

Beware of those mermaids, I told Elise. Turns out a child like her doesn't hear an old woman like me. Have you seen her in the papers? She's been on the front page for a week.

"Did she run away from home? Do we have predators in our neighborhoods? [Continued on page four.]"

Love is what's happening, Mr. Newspaper Man. You won't understand anything about this—too focused on what's probable, aren't you? The *facts*. I'll write your front-page story for you. Sit down and take that pen cap out of your mouth. It goes like this:

"Six days ago, down at the Woods Pond, Elise Franklin, 13, was eaten by mermaids. Numerous times, she had been warned not to go there by the Wise and Unheard Miss Rose. HOWEVER, the child was fool enough to ignore warnings. You see how that goes."

It was love, you know. Why she went there. When it comes to mermaids, it's always love. That last day she came across my bridge, she was silly, beacon-eyed, in full bloom. We've been having talks since she was little, five or six, Matthew's age, and she was never like that. She was a good girl, obedient, pretty. That's what she's known for, her prettiness. That's why she got on the front page.

I was in the creek doing laundry, and she came waving this twiggy branch, singing and full of love shine.

She said, "Miss Rose, you know what? You're wrong. Everything you told me is a lie." Her branch tapped the bridge rail. "You said they were monsters. But I went to the pond and saw them. One with lavender cheeks sang a song just for me." And she stroked her neck.

I shouldn't have yelled. But I did. "That's just the beginning; don't you get it?"

And I threw my dress, soaps and all, into the creek and waded toward her.

"Most of your life, I've been warning you about them. Remember the lost hunter? I watched him slip down their throats. Each of the five, swallowing each of his limbs. And the one who ate his head, that was *my* mermaid. But no, you can't hear me. I don't get to spare anyone else from my life's lot."

I didn't stop there. I wish I would have. Instead, "I'm stronger than you," I said. "I got away. But for the life of me, I don't think you would!"

Of course, she took it as a challenge. I am not easy to get along with. And there they were with lavender cheeks, singing siren songs. Elise scowled and whipped her branch across the water.

"They love me like they never loved you. Who could ever love you?"

Her feet clattered across the bridge. I stood dripping on the bank, watching her sleek long blond hair sway side to side as she ran out of reach and turned a corner between the trees.

You see the part I played.

It makes a woman wonder, what's the point? Of warnings, friendships, confessions about the scars on body and soul.

Have I showed you my scars? Take a look at my skinny hip. Mm-hmm. You see the teeth-marks, don't you? This purple crescent moon scar shapes my left hip. Bet you'd think I'd hate the monster that did that to me. Yet here I am. The farthest I could get away was this bridge—a mile and a half's distance from the pond, following the creek. I have to protect myself and stay away, but we're always connected by this water. It may be the bite-marks that keep me bound to them. Maybe there's a chip of tooth under my skin, trying to get back to its owner.

Here's what I never told the children who visit, not Elise who's gone, not Little Matthew who returns like a boomerang each time I shoo him: I escaped that mermaid over 40 years ago, but a trade occurred. I became an unfinished puzzle. My empty spot matches the shape of her teeth, and she's got my side. It's like a marriage, the way we fit together. And from that day on, I've been filled with secrets and paradoxes, and the fury of loving the ones who wish to devour me.

I never told Elise I love the mermaids, too. Maybe she would've listened better. What do you think, Mr. Newspaper Man? Do people want the whole truth, or edited-for-time-and-clarity truth? Don't answer, just think. How many paradoxes have you trimmed down? How many lives could you've saved by being brave enough to give unclear answers?

Here's some confusion for you. They used to be purely wonderful, in the way of all addictive and otherworldly love affairs.

Knowledge needs to be shared, so I tell Matthew, "Here's a history lesson. Cop a squat."

He brushes his hair sideways across his forehead, sits down on the bank in a tidy pretzel knot, and looks up. I pace the length of the bridge as I lecture, my hair swinging against my cheeks.

"Long ago, mermaids started out the angels of the sea," I say. "They found lost sailors and castaways, breathed in their mouths, kissed their open lips, and loved them strong all their days."

Matthew swivels his head like an owl, watching my course.

"Then the world changed. Navigation improved, also communication. The offerings of the lost went away. So, the mermaids moved inland to small bodies of water. They waited and waited for someone to rescue, and their love got frustrated, and their teeth got sharp.

"They hungered until love became a goal, not what's shared. Now desire owns them, and all they want is more love to fill them. They've lost the understanding of Other—now they're so hungry, they believe they deserve more than anyone should ever get." I stop and raise an eyebrow. "They'll kill you, seriously. Just like they got Elise."

"What happened to Elise?" he asks, which is frustrating because here I've been explaining.

But he's only six, so I spell it out. "Elise went to the pond, where the mermaids swim and sing. They called her close, they pulled her in, and then they ate her."

Little Matthew stops jiggling the stones in his hand, stops everything, and stares at me with fish eyes.

I tuck a tangled gray lock behind my ear. "It's true," I say and flick some dirt from my fingernail.

He funnels his hand and pours the pebbles through, then sweeps the pile flat. "Miss Rose," he says with scrunched mouth, "my mom said if you lie, you go to hell."

This gets me laughing so hard, I'm hacking. I have to spit before I can answer, "I've seen hell already, but that's not what I'm talking about. I'm trying to tell you the truth. One realm of hell is having no one believe you, especially when what you have to say is important."

Matthew ambles over to the creek. Bent like a turtle, he pokes a stick in the muddy bank and makes a neat pattern of holes.

"No one knows what happened to Elise," he says. "My brother said all week she hasn't been in school, and she's not the runaway type. If they don't find her soon, they're going to send out a search party."

His holes line three feet of the bank. He straightens up, admiring them.

Matthew doesn't believe me about the mermaids. He never has. He's six, young, and still confident that he knows everything. Elise was 13. Thirteen, now, that's different. At 13, a girl enters a crossroads, and the various arms of the world reach for her from every direction. But at six, a child is master. He has not yet been swindled by life; he isn't desperate for something better.

• • •

Months ago, Little Matthew found a whole collection of teeth on a slick algae stone. He thought they were from a prehistoric fish that lived in the great age of dinosaurs, back when real monsters existed everywhere, even in our backwoods pond.

He tied up the teeth with yarn and tape and made a wind chime. When their razor edges clinked together in the breeze, high-chiming like faeries, he was dazzled. He hadn't yet heard the mermaids sing like an intoxicating dream, songs that make you yearn, bring you to your knees, and make you wish you never had to return to the dissonant world again. (And the mermaids can arrange this.)

I told him his finding's origin, as the ivory baubles flashed.

"You see, mermaids grow layers of teeth, replacements. When the new rows come in, for a while they have two sets, like sharks, till the old ones fall out. Their little teeth are razor-sharp triangles, and some are chipped from biting through who knows what, a metal dog collar or someone's molars."

I pointed to an uneven one.

He giggled, like I was telling an old woman joke, pulling his leg with a faerytale. I gestured the jagged rows of teeth in a mermaid's mouth, and he chortled like a percolator, shaking his head.

"Mermaids are beautiful," he said, sitting up straight like a schoolteacher. "They have long hair, and a fish tail, and sing on the rocks out at sea. And they're nice. They don't have monster teeth."

He touched the wind chime to make it sing and cut his finger on a tooth.

"Ah, but they're ravenous," I said, swabbing iodine on his finger. "From a distance, so lovely. Up close ... Well see, there you go. The ones who know are here no more."

He admired his red finger, before he faced me. "Then how do *you* know?"

"I got away," I said, and twisted the iodine cap on tight. "I'm the only one I know of. Here's the proof; look at my skinny hip."

I pulled up my dress hem to show him the bite-mark.

His small eyebrows shot up, and he squinted at my wrinkles. My ragged purple scar didn't surprise him. "Ah, that's just 'cause you're old," he explained and looked away.

"There's some sharp eyesight," I said, pulling my hem back down. "Little boy. Believe whatever you want. Just remember the warnings."

And I left him alone with his compliments, because I had better things to do. I figured he'd follow, the boomerang. I picked up the tall bucket I'd prepared for the wolves that morning and pushed past a thin branch at the trailhead.

"Ow," Matthew whispered when the let-go branch caught his face. "Where are we going?"

I filed past the red-skinned young willows lining the path, then waded through the tall meadow grass to the clearing. With my perfected technique, I shimmied the fish from the bucket evenly across the low, flat boulder. My steps donked the empty pail as I walked to a stump out of the way. Matthew sat like a pretzel at my feet, and we watched.

When the first wolf ambled in, he spotted us and crouched, ears back, ready to run. Matthew squeezed my ankle tight but didn't say a word. After a minute, the dark wolf trotted to the stone. He was devouring fish by the time the next two wolves, with black and white markings, entered the meadow—so silently emerging from between the trees, I didn't hear a leaf break. They met our eyes, dropped their hindquarters, and froze.

In Matthew's vise grip, I could feel him counting, three wolves, and two of us. The newcomers stayed stock-still, and then the fishy smell convinced them. Noses twitching, they joined their brother at the feast, and quick-right ate every fish scrap. Then they turned around still chewing, shot us a piercing look, and loped away.

Back at the creek, Matthew jumped in and kicked high fan splashes. "We're friends with the wolves!" he yowled at the sky.

"I wouldn't exactly say friends." I threw a stone at a floating leaf and both sank out of sight.

He kicked again. "Why?"

"Really, we don't know the wolves, and they don't know us. But I gift them fish. They're honorable creatures, loyal to their packs. Me, they recognize and trust enough to eat in front of, but I can't swear they'd call me a friend."

"Why not?"

"Because I'm not a wolf. So, I'll always be different."

Matthew frowned. He kicked around in the water some more, whispering to himself about wolves. When he got bored, he collected his things at my bridge.

"Well, I'm friends with the wolves!" he called as he slowly walked away, holding the wind chime by its string's top loop, careful to keep it away from him.

• • •

Elise wasn't abducted, like Matthew read on the front page; she ran away. She'd risk losing family and friends for one good dose of the love the mermaids have to give. Because when they said, "Let our love make us one," they meant it. One body, filled with the other one.

In the woods, Elise was a cloud-singer, head back serenading the sky, dancing down the trails. I've heard that in town, she went to dances, helped at fairs, making friends while she sold peach cobbler.

You might wonder why she'd risk it all for love when it seemed like she already had it. But there are different kinds, of course. Elise had people telling her they loved her hair, or her smile, or the way she baked them treats.

That's different from being with someone in a world of privacy, with a being made of magic, who loves you because you are you and no other, one who sings praises of *You, You, You,* and *Us*. And the rest of the world could evaporate, but this beautiful creature would still be looking in your eyes, delighted.

I think everyone longs for that. To be taken seriously. To be taken. To trust another so much that you hand yourself over for their safe-keeping. It's an intoxicating dream. And dangerous. It makes you shut your eyes and float, like in your mother's arms, and anything can happen then.

I started out in the city, like most people. I was good and normal, with a job at the dry cleaner's. From ages 14 to 18, I worked the counter. And I had a family that played a family game that never seemed to stop. It involved keeping to a script and smiling, but I was never very good at it. I wasn't abandoning much when I wandered here into the woods. No one noticed me much unless I lost a phone message or the dry cleaning was late.

On the other hand, the mermaids didn't even have clothes. They were naked with iridescent scales, long hair, and eyes that loved me, that didn't ask for anything, except my most essential life.

And if you are going to ask someone for something... After a while it's an insult to only be asked for what anyone could give: change for a dollar, to listen and obey. In a way, it's an honor to be asked for your most precious parts that only you could give.

At least someone is seeing what you have. At least someone knows the treasures you hold inside. And with what better being to share your wealth than the one who recognizes your value?

All the mermaid did was look me in the eyes and ask for everything.

• • •

Imagine with me. It's late, and you're in the woods alone. That's a full moon above, with quick clouds threading by, like marble. Just ahead, the water's silver and burbling. New leaves spring under your feet, and the humid air feels enchanted.

You sit on a mossy boulder by the water, open your mouth and then release a song more beautiful than any you've sung. In the center of the pond, a head rises. The silhouette woman offers a bell-high harmony. So, you keep on allowing through this song that seems destined to arrive from you. When the clouds pull from the moon, in the new light, she glows like a face on a coin. Your glances touch like static sparks.

Eventually, the spell of a song ends, and a nightingale's left trilling. Maybe it sang with you all the while. Fog crawls over the pond's surface, and she dives underwater. She appears inches away at the pond's edge—hair, long and silvered; eyes, wide and aqua; skin, moonlight-tinted pale green. She stares at you without smiling, and you are so daring. You sit, natural as yourself, and look back. Then she speaks.

"You are perfect," she says. "You're just what I've been waiting for. Dive in, please, and let me love you."

She's not pretending you're anything you're not. I deserve this, you tell yourself, so you remove your dress (for you are already revealed), walk through the mud, and drop in. Go underwater and wave free your floating hair; come up seal sleek as she is.

Then she holds you in her strong arms, traces each inch of your untouched body, and she knows. She knows you are beautiful like no one has ever known before. She scatters moth kisses all over your face, as you float and receive.

She keeps whispering, "I love you with everything I've got." Low clouds staunch the moon's light, and she asks, "Do you trust me?"

Eyes open or closed, it's the same in the dark, so you shut them and say, "Yes."

Your word makes her laugh. She fits against you and kisses you with her tongue so warm and soft. And so it goes on.

Till pain is a lightning bolt. Jolting through you. There's a metal taste, and your mouth is full of blood.

She wipes it tenderly from your chin, and says, "I'm sorry, my love." Moonlight returns and gleams off her teeth, a mouthful of sharp edges. "I didn't mean to. Do you believe me?"

When she strokes your head, you dodge and dive away. She's reaching for you. She's so strong. She keeps catching you, and you're choking.

"I can't help but love you," she sings, her fingers gouging between your ribs, "with everything I've got."

Her mouth opens, and you see only points. Dart fast, slip free, get to the pond's edge, and push up on your hands. And then she gives you such a violent kiss. You're on the bank, guts torn open, shadowed in blood. Roll a few feet from the edge, from where she stays, calling love to you and sobbing through her shark teeth. Try to believe she can't leave the water, as you keep on passing out.

In the cold dawn, fishermen find you and carry you away to be mended, as much mending as can be done. You don't want to say what happened, and your split tongue gives you a reason not to. Though later, when you do tell the story, no one will believe a word you say.

No one has ever seen her but you. As is safest. Still, however events turned, she didn't lie. She loved you more than anyone has loved you, and her loving was like heaven, up until the end.

Thank and mourn, all the years after, the luck that got you away.

Attack makes a bond. That mermaid fed from me, and part of me lives on in her. Of course she loved me. Why else would she try to devour me? I can't seem to leave her behind.

Sometimes at night, the pond's call gets loud, and I draw close and watch them from behind the trees. In a circle, the five mermaids join hands and lift them to the stars, singing about their innocence, these martyrs kept hungry for so long. They grimace and gnash their hundred teeth. I run my tongue back and forth to feel my scar, the one I haven't shown anyone. And no one has kissed me since to find it.

I haven't told Matthew *all* I know about mermaids' teeth. Like what happens when you plant one. In 40 days, it lifts a stalk like a fuzzy clothesline. In 20 more days, it grows a bud, big as a grapefruit. This stretches head-sized, and finally it awakens like a lotus. A hundred violet and blue petals curl open and, in the center's bull's-eye, rests a silver globe. The plant gets up to six feet, tall as a relative, and gives an amber scent that carries on the wind for miles.

See, I tried to raise one once. That was the autumn of the nightingales; they flocked to the woods. By midnight, they'd be drunk and silly from the flower's charming resin, and their performances lasted all night. It took a while to figure out why their songs got quieter.

It was at this time that I found the infestation of sticky webbing under each of my plant's wide leaves. I picked apart a web and, in the center, found a silver oval. This seemed the pest's egg, so I pressed a rock into it, and it crunched. Usually, spider and insect cocoons are soft, so I peeled back the silver lining, and discovered tiny bones.

Nightingales. My flower was eating them, as if it converted trilling birdsongs into sweet haunting scent. The plant ate all of the birds but their skulls and breastbones, which were too thick, I suppose. Bees, butterflies, and hummingbirds, it left alone, even though they flocked to its face and orbited where it grew. But no, the crooning nightingales were the preference of that flower grown from a siren's tooth.

My stomach churned as the woods, once loud as a choir hall, grew quieter and quieter, and the stalk grew thicker with hidden skulls and breastbones. Death never smelled so alluring.

Now, we all have responsibilities, and I aim to be a protector. So, with the songbirds in mind, I took to my sword. Years ago, its hilt had poked up from the creek bank, and under the mud and rust, I found lilies engraved down its blade. I wielded this weapon over my shoulder, faced off with the horrible monster I'd grown, and struck down on its bright fragrant head.

It cried piercingly when the flower's silver center broke, a trilling sad song to break a heart. Its lament hypnotized me, as its lotus-like petals spun like a Ferris wheel, violet, blue, violet, blue.

Yet I remembered what I must do. Cheeks wet, surrounded by its soundtrack, I lifted the sword again and hacked at the beguiling flower, chopping it to pieces to end the unearthly song.

Finally, it lay in a heap of ragged ends—petals, plum and navy, scattered on the ground like a kaleidoscope's view. I reached into the center's cracked silver oval and pulled out the sharp mermaid tooth.

It wiggled between my fingers like it was trying to cut me, so I carefully pinched it, hurried to the pond, and threw it back in. Butterflies and hummingbirds followed me, bumping against my perfumed hands, mournfully circling the air. They stayed a long time, gyring above the water, searching for the magnet that had controlled their days.

• • •

Little Matthew tells me about the town's search party. Up and down the highway, he says, troops of local men look for Elise, and each day her picture is on the newspaper's front page.

Today, the men tromp through the woods with big rifles and little walkie-talkies, orange vests, and camouflage caps. They bark orders and survey the pond, but it's calm there. Mermaids go underwater on sunny days. They're more night-beings, like barn owls and cat snakes—and besides, in the sunlight, they're a pale green tint or blue, shining like mica. If they stood still, you'd never mistake a shape that color for a person's head rising from the water.

The search party hunts all day, but they don't find Elise, or the mermaids. Later on that night, the mermaids find me. They come in a dream that isn't only a dream, but a happening that occurs while I'm asleep.

Improbable beauties crowd around my bedroll. I know I'm asleep because they stand on the tips of their tails, needing no water. Five swiveling ladies reach down sleek arms, and their hands swim over me like starfish, stroking my hair and neck.

"Aren't you hungry," ring their bell voices. "Hungry for so much."

"Your body's old. It holds you back," their voices spin. "But we know you're lovely," lips moving, words overlapping.

"Come with."

"Be one."

"We know you," they say, and these last words don't echo, and then they quietly stroke my loose skin and wonder over my old legs. They take my swollen knees like grapefruits in their palms and stick fingers between my toes. I try to curl up, but they hold my limbs and slowly straighten them.

Each one is stunning in her way. Shafts of moonlight stream under the bridge and paint them with glowing abstract shapes. My mermaid who tried to devour me, she of the wide aqua eyes, bends down and examines my knotted calves and blue-vein thighs.

"You could trade these for a powerful tail, my sweet," she says. "Walking hurts, doesn't it. Why struggle when the water can support you?"

"Leave the world behind."

"Dirty, heavy world."

And it's true the world's weight presses me down. This superficial world under a greedy spell, it's a steel anvil laid on my chest, and I thrash to get out from beneath it.

I chose the woods instead of the city's prizes, this bridge and my moss-stuffed bedroll. I keep a lifestyle where my pace is free. I can watch the sunlight shift and the seasons' changes and know what I know about the world, without anyone calling me a liar. But it is lonely.

"You are the only one," their voices ring, "worthy… worthy… hungry… As us."

Each visitor to the woods leaves more trash, cans and gun shells and oil spills on the ground. Their carelessness unfurls in all directions, riding my shoulders, heavy and unstoppable. It sure would be nice to plunge into water, float, dream, and give in, get filled. I could be a creature of wild desire, too, untouched by age, breathing water and easy to love.

My face stretches with a smile, till, "No!"

I thrash from my own convincing.

Then they're gone, the ambassadors of the wicked offer. The sunlight's bright; a chipmunk runs across my foot. I sit up in the next day of the familiar life and rub my aching knees.

Half a sprite-face watches me from a lilac bush. Matthew rises with a pollen puff in his hair, then sits on the rock next to me, thinking deeply, slouching and breathing loud.

"Do you think it hurt when the mermaids ate Elise?" His hawk eyes pierce the clear sky.

"I don't know," I say, and my fingers press the soil.

He faces me. "Did it hurt when they bit you?"

My nerves get a lightning strike. He's never believed me before.

"She. It was only one of them," I say. My palm fits against the moist ground.

"Did it hurt?" he keeps asking.

"Yes."

"Yes," he repeats, like the word is sacred. And he's quiet for a long while.

I don't know if this is how I'm supposed to talk to children. I guess most people just tell them good-sounding lies so they won't cry. But what's the point of that? It just makes them fall harder when the letdown comes.

Next time I look at Little Matthew, he has his forearm in his mouth and is biting down hard.

"Stop that!" I yell, and swat him.

He bursts out crying and runs away.

I never said I was good with children.

"Miss Rose."

Two search party men stop to talk to me on their return trip from the woods. "When's the last time you saw Elise?"

The security guard, Tom, knows about me and my bridge, like the other town folk; my family are his neighbors. People don't usually bother me here.

I don't mean to tell him anything. "A little while ago." I keep up with my work.

The short one, Mikey, his mechanic's shirt says, keeps swallowing like he just took a pill without water. He clenches his hands, staring at the bowl between my knees.

"When exactly is 'a little while ago?'" Tom asks.

I sift through the dry grain, pick out a bug, and toss in to the little bug pile.

"The moon went from dark to past first quarter. What's that? Eight days," I say.

Mikey runs his fingers through his hair and makes it greasy.

"I haven't seen the girl since new moon." When I spit, Mikey flinches hard, though it lands far from him.

Tom clears his throat. "And what were you doing the last time you saw Elise?"

I dig in and grab another palmful of grain.

"Laundry," I say. "She crossed my bridge on her way to the woods. Told me a song she'd made up. Then she left."

Tom's excited. "And did you see her come back across?"

"No," I say, and I tell him more, but he's already heard enough.

Who could have guessed my interview's effects? Tom uses it as the keystone evidence for his theory.

1. Elise went into the woods and never came out.

2. Something in the woods killed her.

3. A sheriff spotted a wolf pack crossing the road and entering the woods.

4. The biggest local danger, which the men will now eradicate, is—

Wolves.

And so the hunting begins.

The town's men enter the land in great snarling packs. Guns fire, creating an audible map of how far the woods extend. Birds stop singing and everything quiets, except for the pack of men. At night they return, and flashlight beams swing through the trees' branches. Rays of light and bending tree silhouettes steal my night vision.

Come morning, Tom and three others cross my bridge with shotguns. My mouth opens, and I can't help but yell a heartfelt croaking lecture about how few wolves are left here anymore and how they avoid humans. As the men keep walking, I shout curses. Tom stops for just a moment, when he turns toward me and takes aim.

Little Matthew lingers around my bridge, heavy and serious. His eyes carry dark bags, and he doesn't play around. When he finally speaks, it's in a high voice.

"I know you said you're not friends with the wolves, but you are—admit it. You feed them, and you know they didn't get Elise. So why do they have to die?"

I say words to explain what can't be understood. "Those hunters won't hear me. They're going to do this."

"How could they?" he asks.

His heart is breaking, and I've no duty to defend those brutes. Yet look at him needing to know.

So, I say, "My guess is they're scared. They love their kids, and they're afraid of losing them. They want to protect them, but they don't know who's after them, so they chose to kill the wolves." I say, "Sometimes love makes people do horrible things, out of fear. Do you understand?"

"No," he says.

"Lord knows it doesn't make sense," I say, "but it's what I've seen is true."

"What do you know?" he says, angry. "You're crazy, Miss Rose. You don't know anything and you never did."

Matthew walks away, hitting each tree branch he passes, believing he is all alone and the first person to feel this way.

I'm snapping pebbles at a tree trunk when, BOOSH, a heavy wind comes gusting into the late afternoon. My stones fly far off mark. Within the roaring air, I hear a muffled gunshot. A dead branch cracks off a tree behind me, flies by. It misses my nose by an inch, and smacks my pebbles' tree trunk target, right on bull's-eye. The branch lands like a tambourine, clattering leaves.

The wind builds to a scream, and you'd never believe it was calm until a moment before. My skin's lined in goosebumps, my hair stands on end, and I *know* this kind of sudden bluster.

This is the Wind of Change. You live long enough, paying attention, and you see patterns. The turning wind blows in before weather-snaps, and it gusts just the same before life's changes—beginnings, endings, births, deaths. Prescience fills me like a fog full of static cling, and I can feel that *something* is happening, but not what. The wolves?

Little Matthew. At once, I pull toward him (*They can't take another one*) like a compass arrow pointing north.

No time for second-guesses. A gunshot cracks the air, followed by a wolf cry. I bustle my long dress and discover how fast an old woman can run in the woods against the wind. Weeds lash my legs, and the world is all rattling leaves and ghostly wind-cries.

When I get to the pond, leaves and dirt pepper the air, and I peer through my eyelashes. The trees surrounding the clearing bow and raise like waves, and the pond is like dented metal. I spot his little brown crown on the far bank, so I race along the bank, strong and furious, and thunder to a stop.

Little Matthew sits away from the pond's edge, against the wall of tangled growth. And nothing seems to be wrong.

"You scared the life out of me!" I shout, wheezing, and drop next to him in the grass. "What are you doing here? I told you to stay away."

Strangely calm, Matthew sits, his shirt rippling in the wind.

"I wanted to kill them," he says, "or do I-don't-know-what to those mermaids, for eating Elise, and making the men hunt the wolves. I was going to keep away from the water. I heard the guns and the wolves howling. It was loud, and I yelled, 'Come out, you murderers!' And even though I'd started believing you, I didn't see any mermaids in that pond, and I started thinking you were just a big liar." He slowly shakes his head.

An uncanny shift takes over as Little Matthew tells his story, because the Matthew inside his tale is vivacious and hot-cheeked, yet the one reciting next to me has a face calm as the moon. Expressionless, he watches the setting of his tableau.

I face the churning pond also, imagining along with him:

At the water's edge, Matthew is little but fearless, a thin boy screaming curses. Then, a mermaid rises from the water, and she tells him, "Shh." She says, "I hear you." And somehow, her voice speaks an inch from his ear. The boy stands defiantly on the bank, as two more mermaids rise from the pond. "It's okay," they tell him, and they are magnificent, not monsters like I said. Their long hair is in many braids, and their iridescent skin glitters. The boy shakes his fists, condemning the men hunting the wolves, decrying the injustice.

How can he stand it? the mermaids ask him. "I don't know," he admits. So, they sing a grace-note melody about running with the wild wolves, and gold sunshine on his back, about being loved. Their voices are high as faery chimes, and it's the prettiest moment, he says, he's ever lived. One of the mermaids holds up a red, shiny rock. "Here is our love," she tells the boy, like their love is a red rock he can put in his pocket. When he bends down to see it closer, a wolf zooms by behind his legs.

Matthew gestures the swoop. "Then there was a loud gunshot." He wakes from his trance and seems a little surprised to see me.

"Did you take the stone?" I ask.

"No, I ran into the woods so I wouldn't get shot. And I thought if I saw a mermaid? That would be a message that I'm safe and don't have to worry. But I waited a long time and didn't see one, so then I came out anyway. That's when I found the wolf. He's dead. I wanted to stay with him."

We sit alone by the pond.

"Where is he?" I ask.

"Right here," Matthew says, turning around. He stands and searches. "There he is!" He points with a straight arm.

From a gap in the trees, a wolf emerges, and blood mats half his fur from his belly's bullet hole.

"He's not dead!" Matthew cries.

Long strands of saliva drip, as the wolf snarls.

"He's one of the ones we fed!"

Ten feet before us, the wolf plants his feet and howls terribly loudly, three times, like a ritual.

"Matthew, shh."

I puff out my chest and try to look imposing. The wolf's eyes shine with pain, and he yelps, then growls like a nightmare. His unbloodied fur bristles like static electricity, and he crouches, preparing to spring. Then a second wolf joins him, jogging out from the wall of trees. His monochrome twin licks his back, and I recognize her, but not her curled lip or snapping jaws.

I'm already retreating when the wounded wolf leaps. My tripping feet run backward, and then there's a white blur flying through the air. A cloud of small white triangles glitters past. I protect my head with a bent arm, and when the brief cloud clears, I find the wounded wolf in death throes on the ground. His eye streams blood, and his legs sprawl.

It happens too fast to understand. The she-wolf howls like she's calling to the gods, and she gives a jaw-snap. She squats, shifting feet, then charges us.

Again, the air glitters with a white swarm. I see pale shards sink into the wolf's leg and belly fur. The wolf falters but uses her remaining strength for a last leap.

Her paws land on my shoulders, and she stands, staggering, breathing in my face like we're lovers embracing; our wild eyes meet.

The air fills with shards once more, and the wolf cries, dropping from me with a thump, growl, and gurgle. Then she is silent, a pile of fur on the ground.

I wait beside Matthew, knees bent, but nothing else charges. After three killing swarms of white shards blurring past us, not one touched me. Little Matthew shivers, but he's unhurt. Arms hugging himself tight, he stands above the wolf and looks down at her death. Her thick fur tosses up and down in the wind.

"I didn't want them to die," he whispers.

My hair swirls in front of my eyes like a question mark. I turn to face the wind, and there's my mermaid. She grips the pond's rim and watches me with lovely eyes, and I am nothing but inhale.

Then, she smiles, and her lips curve around a black hollow. Toothless, she looks old, like me. She lifts her hand, gentle, to touch her mouth, and when her fingers leave the water, they streak with blood. It was her teeth that killed the wolves, I realize. She broke them out and threw them like a dagger swarm.

"Why did you help us?" I call, my voice sounding unused.

She gives an empty smile and descends beneath the water.

Was it love? Protection? Or jealousy. Could she not stand to see an object of obsession taken by another?

I imagine it's love, and my chest warms like there's a palm laid on it. After all that's happened, she still loves me. Closer I come and peer down into the green, choppy waves. I don't know how to thank her, so I just bend down and pet the water a little, like it's her soft cheek. It must have hurt her to break out all her teeth.

But they'll grow back.

Her hand darts up. Reflexively, I withdraw, and her long nails slash the air. I shuffle back from the pond. And grimacing, she rises, reaching out for me.

"Don't go," she sings with her eyes closed. She doesn't aim to catch me, but she can't stop trying.

A safe distance away, I sit on a lichen-spotted boulder and watch her blind swipes. After a good while, I clear my throat and say, "I'm here."

Then she sinks below the water and is gone. I track the dent she leaves in the surface.

"Didn't you see," Little Matthew says, touching my back. "That mermaid didn't have shark teeth—she didn't have any teeth at all."

A zephyr blows through, and the gray sky breaks with streaks of fuchsia dusk.

"It was just a little red rock," he tells me. "Like a pebble." And casually, he untangles my hair with his small hand.

■

Dawn Sperber is a writer and freelance editor, based New Mexico. Most of her writings focus on healing and magic in some way, though the ways change. Her stories and poems have appeared in NANO Fiction, PANK, Hunger Mountain, Gargoyle, Going Down Swinging, The Doctor T. J. Eckleburg Review, We'Moon, *and elsewhere. Learn more at dawnsperber.com.*

SMILE

— ∎ —

William Basso

I grew up in a household where both of my parents were artists, so as a child I was surrounded by all types of art from all periods in history, on the walls, in art books, etc., and was also exposed to museums and galleries on a regular basis. I received a BFA degree in illustration from Parson's School of Design in New York City, but I decided to pursue a career in special effects and character makeup for the film industry. I've always loved movies, especially horror, fantasy and science fiction. This made for a rich foundation resulting from not only the influences of my artistic home surroundings but also my own imagination sparked by the pulp fantasies of pop culture. So of course for me it made sense to move to Los Angeles and get into the movie business. After almost twenty years working in films I became interested in exploring my own point of view and began producing personal art. I now live and work in New Jersey.

I would classify my work as mixed-media. I use the camera and the computer as artistic tools like any other. I typically begin a piece by drawing and working out ideas on paper. This is followed by sculpting and constructing a series of miniature, doll-like characters or maquettes, as well as a variety of intricate handmade objects that I then photograph. My photographs are then processed in the computer along with my scanned drawings. Each composition is made up of a number of these visual fragments, all edited using Adobe Photoshop software. I print out sections of my imagery, and using collage techniques, build what will become the final assemblage. The printed pieces are cut, torn, altered, rearranged, etc. The work is constructed with these layers of printed imagery, as well as paint mediums and other media on a panel. Although I usually have a definite composition worked out, the piece evolves and changes as aesthetic passages are revealed. My purely sculptural work is created much like the working maquettes described above but taken to a more complete state.

I think that my work is partially influenced by the past, from things like early cinema, art history, curiosity cabinets and early photography, for example. I'm interested in exploring my own subconscious, a dream world that exists somewhere between a childlike sense of fantasy and adult anxieties. I often draw inspiration from more primitive technologies. Things made with gears, ropes and wooden planks. A hand made feeling. My working methods also have an influence on the theatrical flavor of the pieces, in that I'm creating and working with various fabricated objects and handmade characters. As I'm working, it can feel as though I'm staging a tiny theater piece or perhaps curating a mysterious museum exhibit combined with a long ago forgotten sideshow of curiosities.

My work has been exhibited in a number of galleries around the country as well as being featured in both the SPECTRUM fantastic arts annuals and The Society of Illustrators art annuals.

www.basso-art.com